HAUNTED BY THE PAST

Friends In Crisis Series (Book I)

Lucy Appadoo

This book is dedicated to victims of bullying and violence. It is also dedicated to my husband and two daughters who always give me the space to write.

Contents

Chapter One

A NEW VENTURE

In the back courtyard of Bella Carismo's cottage-style brick home, three women celebrated the Friday evening and sipped Bordeaux. The setting sun glinted off their wine glasses.

"It's great that you guys want to help but I just need more time," Bella said. She peered into her wine with fidgeting hands and wondered if she was even good enough to attract more clients into her counselling practice. She was not great at marketing, given her introverted nature.

The wind howled as Bella shared a laugh with Liz and Jamie, the effects of the wine simmering in her body like the warmth of a gentle fire. The spring air smelled of post-rain dampness and freshly cut grass.

Liz shook her head and laced her long-dainty fingers around her wine glass. She was barely able to fit on the white, plastic chairs due to her tall, lanky figure. Her smiling hazel eyes and jet-black hair made her all the more striking. Liz radiated confidence and filled up the space with her presence. "I know it's only been a few months since starting your counselling practice, but I'm happy to help now." She gave Bella a reassuring smile. "If you want to expand it, hand me your business cards and I'll talk to my connections at the centre. The other social workers there might know of people who need counselling."

"I can do that. Sure," Bella said.

Jamie flicked a wave of short red hair, settling comfortably into her chair due to her short stature and average build. She smilingly handed Bella a long list of tasks, her grin softening the usual searing intensity of her brown-eyed gaze. "I'm happy to give you a list of priority tasks that you can start with. Firstly, I'd begin with contacting all the local doctors, and then you can hand out your cards at the local community centre. Then perhaps do a book signing for your book. I've actually already made a list for you." She stretched out her right arm and handed Bella an A4 piece of paper with a long list of tasks.

Bella's shoulders slouched. "I guess I'll have to do that sort of thing, even if I hate doing it. At least I have a website and advertise on social media."

Liz gave her an encouraging smile. "I know it's hard, Bella, but you have to do those things to help you expand. You need to get yourself out there and make yourself known, be a presence in the Williamstown community. I can help you do that. The best way is through networking. Get out of your shell, girl."

Bella remained silent as the wind quieted down and darkness settled over them. She sipped the remaining drops of her wine and stared out over the tropical trees dancing in the air above her high timber fence.

Bella had opened her own counselling practice three months ago. She had inherited the money from her late aunt Faye, who had died a year ago of an aggressive cancer, and Bella used the money to buy a small, quaint building for her new business.

Liz interrupted her thoughts. "Anyway, I say that whatever you decide, don't take too long. This is your full-time job now and it does take a fair bit of marketing until you can make a name for yourself. I mean unless you want to go back to your dragon employer."

Bella shook her head. "No, thanks. I'll do just fine where I am."

Jamie took hold of her hand. "I think that you can look at my tasks at your own pace. Don't rush through it. Take it one baby step at a time. I don't want you to feel overwhelmed with all this. We are here to help you. If you need financial assistance, please let me know."

Liz brought her caviar dip topped cheese cracker to her mouth. She wiped stray crumbs after devouring it. "Anyway, back to other exciting things, Bella. I've been invited to a party celebrating my colleague's twenty years at the centre. She's asked me to bring my friends, so you are going to come, right? Please don't say no like you usually do."

Bella's stomach flipped. "I'll think about it, but you know I hate celebrations."

Liz touched her on the shoulder. "Look, I know that stuff with your dad was cruel. You should probably talk to someone about it."

Bella nodded, pushing down her thoughts of her father. "I will, but after all this crazy stuff with the business settles down."

Liz cleared her throat. "I promise you it'll be fun. Just a few people, not too crowded."

Jamie interrupted. "Leave it alone, Liz. If Bella doesn't feel comfortable going to this celebration, then leave her out of it. You will have me there."

"Hmmm," said Liz.

Bella looked fondly at Jamie. *God Bless Her*! She shuddered. If only Bella could put the past behind her and move on with her life, she'd be a happier person.

Chapter Two

AMBIGUITY

Early Saturday morning, Bella stretched out her arms. She yawned, lifted off the quilt cover, and got out of bed to begin her strict routine. The room was minimally furnished with a round timber bedside table and desk lamp, bay windows featuring Venetian blinds, and a small armoire. She moved to the study opposite her bedroom, stepping onto the cold floorboards with her bare feet. She bowed down and sat against a wall with her back pressed against a cushion, a large feather-down pillow to sit on, and another smaller pillow to rest her legs. Closing her eyes, she meditated for twenty-minutes.

Bella rose and prepared breakfast, then showered. As she moved towards the living room, she picked up her laptop from the round coffee table with a range of "Psychology Today" subscriptions stacked in an orderly pile and rested back on her tan leather couch. A smart TV was built into the wall and a cabinet sat below it. She looked fondly at the photograph of her aunt Faye on it every morning. The photo reminded her of the bond they'd shared when her aunt was alive.

Bang! Muffled voices echoed nearby. She flinched at the noise. *Probably, the neighbours,* she thought. *Nothing to worry about.* She was being silly again. Williamstown could be loud at times. There was no point in checking out every noise.

She turned on her laptop and waited for it to boot up. Clicking on her email, Bella waited for messages, hoping that she had enquiries from her social media advertisement. She worked mainly with adults who presented with a range of issues including stress management, depression, anxiety, anger management issues, and some types of personality disorders. Bella realised that even normally functioning people experienced mental health issues on some level, but they were able to manage them.

Mostly junk mail filled her inbox, some of which she unsubscribed from. One of them had the subject line, *You Don't Have a Clue.* Out of curiosity, she opened the email.

To the questionable psychologist,

I saw your advertisement about your new counselling practice and am intrigued. Can you really help people when you're such a loser? Don't get too cocky in your new business. I doubt it'll last long.

Bella pulled at her hair and took deep breaths in an effort to calm herself. She closed the email and paced across the rug, her bare feet hardly feeling the warmth and thickness of the fabric. She clenched her hands and fought back images of self-doubt. *It was just a stupid email!* Her advertisement was bound to attract the unstable. There were plenty of them in the world. She should've known her advertisement would attract the wrong kinds of people.Maybe this person was bored, with nothing better to do than getting their kicks out of upsetting people. It could also have been a prankster who wanted her reaction. Well, she wouldn't react to trolls as they were plentiful. It was just a spam message with no real significance. She was letting it get to her, making her mouth dry and her stomach feel heavy.

Bella decided to leave the email where it was. She'd deal with it later. She got ready for her Tai Chi class. Every Saturday, she had Tai Chi as it was a sport that gave her a sense of security. She'd been attending for the past year and savoured the freedom of movement and the way it relaxed her.

It was silly to worry about a stupid email message that probably meant nothing. She gave it no more thought as she picked up her bag and car keys and headed out the door.

As she walked outside, her kindly elderly neighbour, Beatrice, was watering her roses in the front garden. She had been a widow for the past year, and Bella had spent the odd occasion having tea with her in her home.

The short woman with grey hair and prominent wrinkles waved. "Hello, dear. Going out?"

"Hi, Beatrice. Yes, my Tai Chi class."

"Have a lovely day. Don't forget to come by for tea soon."

She smiled. "Of course. I'll let you know. See you later."

"Goodbye, dear Bella."

Bella stepped into her white Toyota Corolla parked at the front of her house. She opened her window, turned on the motor and was ready to drive off.

The alert that the email had been opened popped up on the phone screen. A few minutes later, Bella stepped outside and into her small car. *I'm going to make your life a living hell, bitch!* Bella wasn't worth the ground she walked on. *I'll take my time with you. Nice and slow. No mercy.* Bella was going to get the biggest surprise of her life. The cell phone dropped onto the passenger seat. Bella's car disappeared around the corner. *Time to make Bella pay, for everything.*

Chapter Three

A VISITOR

Bella fiddled with the lock on the door. Her shoulders slumped, sighing at the dreaded Monday morning. It took her a while to get going, but she'd be fine later in the day.

The grey building had red awnings above the windows with a sign to the right that displayed, *Bella's Counselling Services.* The building was in the middle of Williamstown, close to Bella's favourite bookshops and retail stores.

She unlocked the front door and stepped inside. The interior of the building was well-furnished with its white-washed walls. A waiting area greeted her, filled with a mixture of small armchairs and plastic chairs, magazines, and business cards piled on a glass tabletop. There was a rug covering the floorboards in the waiting area. Above the reception counter on the wall, 3D butterfly decals protruded in two rows. Each insect had two pastel colours. The largest was yellow and black. Two butterfly crystal figurines sat on either side of the counter. It had been her receptionist, Mari, who had wanted to bring a bit of colour and vibrancy to greet clients in the area. The butterflies added aesthetic appeal and brightened the place, and Bella was grateful for the decorating idea.

Bella's office contained a white ergonomic chair and a large desk. An array of stationery, a telephone, and manuals lay neatly across the edge of the desk, and a filing cabinet held case files and assessment test results. Diagnostic tools, psychological inventories, and books sat on a towering bookshelf, and her Postgraduate Diploma of Psychology hung on the nearby wall.

Bella almost tripped on the round rug set in the middle of the room. She regained her bearings then hunched over to grab a case file from the cabinet. She placed her bag in a lockable steel cupboard then sat at her desk, peering over the notes of her first client of the day. Bella had time before the client arrived in an hour. Bella's workday would be over by early afternoon as she only had a few bookings. If she didn't find more clients, it would be a struggle financially. She would have to dip into her savings.

Bella turned over the pages. The client had been abused by her violent husband. Luckily, he was in prison now. The woman was slowly learning to manage the flashbacks and nightmares of the abuse. No children involved, thankfully, but it would take her a while to trust another man again.

Bella understood abuse only too well. Her mind took her back to another time, another place, when her old school acquaintance, Bridget Mardot, had called her a few weeks ago wanting to make amends after bullying Bella for years. Her friends, Dawn and June, gave her a few good experiences at school that got her through the bullying. The conversation with Bridget was clear in her head. "Hey, Bella. It's Bridget from high school."

Bella's hand gripped the phone, her breath stopping. "Why are you ringing me?"

"Listen, I know it's been a long time, but I've changed and want to make amends. I feel badly about what I did to you. Can we meet?"

It took Bella a minute to get her head around this. She figured she had nothing to lose. Maybe closure was best. "Okay, where do you want to meet?"

"At the usual cafe the school kids went to close to the port. Say one o'clock next Saturday?"

"Okay, see you then."

Bella hung up with a heavy heart and took a calming breath to fight off the images that had haunted her for years.

She had shown up at the cafe near the port, but Bridget had stood her up. She called her a few times after that, but the call went straight to voicemail. *Typical*. It was probably better this way.

Bella returned to the present. She smiled at the progress her client had made. Initially, the poor woman would cry inconsolably for half of their session. Now, after one month of weekly counselling, she was able to deal with the disturbing images without completely breaking down.

Light footsteps and a voice jolted her out of her reverie. She turned around and smiled at Mari, who only worked with her on a casual basis whenever she had clients booked in, as she couldn't afford to put her on full-time at this stage.

"Hello, Mari."

"Hi, Bella. How are you going with getting more clients?" Her smiling blue eyes drew people in, and her brown hair with copper highlights was damp. Mari mentioned how she was always rushing in the mornings, hence her wet hair. She was twenty-seven years old, the same age as Bella, highly intelligent, nurturing, and efficient in her role as receptionist. Hiring her had been the right decision.

Bella put down her case file and rose. "I have some marketing ideas, and I promise once I can afford to pay you full-time, I will. Bear with me."

Mari nodded. "No worries. I've got my website work that gets me by. Happy to help." She cleared her throat. "I'll let you know when your first client comes in." She waltzed out of the office humming to herself. If only Bella could be that chirpy in the mornings.

Bella walked over to the staff room and picked up a mug. She filled it with coffee, sugar, milk, and then water from the boiling urn before sitting down and sipping it slowly.Mari walked into the room. "I'm sorry to interrupt, Bella, but there's someone here to see you. Her name's Claudia."

Bella's head jerked up from her coffee. A sudden coldness hit at her core and her heartbeat raced. *What more could this woman do to me?* "Thanks, Mari. I'll be out front in a minute." She swallowed and put a hand over her chest, calming her thoughts. *It's all fine. It's all fine. I can handle this.*

She walked back to her office and locked away her case file, then straightened her stationery. Her finger flicked over the desk, and she felt dust lingering. She grabbed a tissue from a box on the shelf and wiped the dust from her desk, careful to clean under the stationery items.

Bella straightened her blouse, took a deep breath, then walked to reception. The woman sat on an armchair, flicking through a magazine. When Claudia saw Bella, her serene expression shifted, and her brows bumped together. Those cold, grey eyes, the rigid strawberry-blonde hair tied up in a bun, and the ash-black business suit made her appear exactly as she was. Aloof and clinical.

Bella forced a smile. "Hello, Claudia. How are you?"

Claudia's eyes raked over her from top to bottom. "Fine. I can see you've made somewhat of a name for yourself."

Bella ignored the flutter in her stomach and regained her breath. "It's still new, but I am doing fine for now."

Claudia peered at her watch then rose from the seat. Her eyes flickered over to Mari. "Is there any chance of some privacy? I have somewhat of a proposition for you."

Bella was sick in the stomach. She couldn't go back there again. She wouldn't.

"What kind of proposition?"

She moved ahead of Bella, searching for her office. "If you don't mind, I'd rather speak in private."

Bella nodded then led her to her office, dawdling a little. Whatever Claudia had to offer, it couldn't be good.

Chapter Four

AN OFFER

Bella wanted to hide under a rock or be at the beach. Anywhere but here right now. This woman was nothing but trouble, but she had to stay on her good side. She sat down while Claudia smoothed out her skirt as she sank down on the chair opposite.

With a resigned sigh, Claudia said, "I'd like you to come back to the practice."

Bella winced and wondered about her ulterior motive. "I already have a job, my business here. But thanks for the offer."

Claudia clasped her hands together and looked around the office with sharp focus. "I guess it's okay here in what you call an establishment, but I thought you might like to make real money. My practice is expanding, and I need extra staff to handle the caseload. I could use your expertise."

Bella peered down at the floor, her feet suddenly feeling constricted in her closed-toe wedge shoes. She fiddled with the collar of her blouse and fought back the images of the time she'd worked for Claudia just over one year ago. Why would she want to return to a toxic work environment again? She'd learnt from her bad choices and couldn't face working with her again. "Thanks for the offer, Claudia, but I'm fine where I am. I'd like to expand my own practice closer to home."

She nodded, but the coldness in her eyes was unmistakable. "I understand but I'm still in Newport, not that far from here. And I'd be willing to offer you a lot more money than what you were previously earning. We're doing well so I can afford it. At least think about it. I'll call you in a few days."

Bella clenched her hands together, nails digging into her skin. She refused to go back to that nightmare. "As I said, I'm fine where I am."

Claudia tapped her foot on the floor, pressing her lips together. "I guess we should make amends for the past. I know I gave you a high caseload and you were burnt out. Then you were attacked by your patient, but I apologised for that. I really am sorry. I see my mistake now and I appreciate how hard you worked, but, in the end, you became less productive. It won't be the same again."

Bella dared to speak the words. "And have you forgotten how that patient who attacked me was your patient beforehand?" It had been the last straw for Bella when she decided to quit. "This client was triggered because of your lack of boundaries. Did you know that? How could you visit his home and get involved in his business and family? He told me all that. He threatened to go to the Psychology Board, but I convinced him otherwise. And what about your other clients? Your lack of boundaries with them too? I imagine you're still doing that. Are you? It's too risky for me to work for you. It could cost me my licence."

Claudia avoided her eyes and shook her head. "No, I realised the error of my ways."

She avoided her eyes. "You can be reported to the PBA, Claudia. You know that."

"And who's going to tell on me? You?"

Bella had considered it once or twice, but she didn't want the stress. She'd had enough stress to deal with in her lifetime. All she wanted was to help people within the boundaries set for clinical psychologists. She looked into Claudia's eyes and knew she was lying. She was still getting overly involved with her clients, and a strong part of Bella wanted to report her to the PBA, but she worried that Claudia might retaliate in some way. She didn't believe she was strong enough to fight Claudia, particularly with her connections to unscrupulous family members who were crooked politicians. Even if Claudia didn't fight back, her family no doubt would. In the end, karma would surely get her.

"No, not me." She took a calming breath. "Did you forget that when I resigned, you told me never to come back to you?"

Claudia rose from her seat, ignoring her comment. "At least give it some thought. I'll contact you in a few days or so."

Bella got up from her chair and walked Claudia out of the office. Mari stared at her quizzically, but she turned her attention again to Claudia and opened the door for her. "Goodbye, Claudia."

Claudia turned around. "How about we say, see you later for now." She handed her a business card. "Here's my number, in case you lost it. But I'll be in touch and hope to get a yes from you. Take care." She took long-legged strides towards her car parked at the kerb.

Bella walked back inside the practice with a heavy heart.

Mari was putting away files in a filing drawer and smiled. "Are you okay, Bella? You look a bit frazzled."

"I'm fine, thanks. Please let me know when my client comes in."

Mari nodded. "Of course."

Bella headed back to her office with a deflated posture and closed her eyes briefly as she reached for the case file of her first client. A strong tremor shook her body as she recalled the day her ex-patient beat her. In spite of her challenging experiences, Bella had been able to create an inner safety net. Her inner demons propped up at times, but she had moved on and was starting to build a new life for herself.

Chapter Five

THE NEW CLIENT

Later that day, Bella grabbed a file from the cabinet. She flicked through the prepared case folder and turned to a lined blank page. She started writing notes for her next client when her phone rang. "Thanks, Mari. I'll be right there." She finished up her notes then walked into the waiting area where her next client stood, green eyes smiling regardless of her sagging posture. "Hi, Sonia. Come on through." The middle-aged woman struggled to walk even with her cane as she followed Bella into her office.

Bella enjoyed working with Sonia. She was a fighter, and optimistic in spite of her challenges.

They took their respective seats while Bella held on to her note pad with pen in hand. "How's your week been, Sonia?"

"Oh, you know, can't complain. John's been a great support with the girls, and I'm lucky to have the support of my boss at work..."

"I sense a but in there somewhere," said Bella.

Sonia smiled. "Even my parents are great in spite of their age, and the girls help out with jobs at home. I only wish I didn't have this damn rheumatoid arthritis. It's a damn curse. I struggle to get out of bed every morning and can't even wash my hair at times. It's embarrassing when my daughter has to wash it because of the pain."

Bella reflected back her pain and frustration until Sonia's mood lifted. "Have you tried the mindfulness meditation exercise and pacing activities we discussed last week?"

"A little, but it's been busy this past week."

"Hmm. Let's create an activity schedule, which works even for busy people." Bella smiled and the woman's posture lifted.

In the last few minutes of the session, Sonia said, "I'm sure you know what I mean about my family always being there for me. I mean, it's not only support, but definitely the right kind of support. That's all I can ask for. I'm lucky to have had an amazing childhood with my family. I'm grateful for that."

Bella ignored the hollowness in her stomach. She ignored the headache and the blurred vision threatening to swallow her whole as she held firm to her client's words. Why couldn't her own parents be like that? Loving and supportive?

After the session, Sonia was a new woman with a spring in her step as Bella showed her to the door. Mari interrupted her. "Oh, you have a message from this man enquiring about counselling." She handed Bella the note with her scrawled handwriting.

"Thanks. I'll call him back."

Mari drew her eyebrows together. "Is everything okay? You look sad."

Bella nodded. "I'm fine. Just tired, that's all."

Mari gave her a reassuring smile as she sealed an envelope and placed it in her in-tray. "All these problems. It must get to you sometimes."

Bella shrugged. "I love the work, and helping people has its own rewards."

"Well, that's good, I suppose."

Bella made her way back to her office and dialled the number of the caller. A flutter rose in her chest. She always got a little nervous speaking to new people. "Hello, is this Jackson?"

"Yes, who's this?"

"This is Bella Carismo, the psychologist. You called my office earlier today to enquire about my services."

"Yes, I need counselling. Can you help me?"

"Can you tell me about your issue?" She waited at least ten seconds before getting a response.

"I don't know. Just anger, I guess."

Bella swallowed. She could hear the tension in his voice. "Can you tell me more about that?" Again, a moment of silence pervaded her. "Jackson?"

"Sorry, aahm. I guess I get a bit aggressive, more verbal, aah...not so physical or anything like that." He didn't sound very convincing to Bella. He went on, "I've tried others but they're too busy right now. You sound pleasant. Can you please make time for me?"

The sound of desperation in his voice made her curious. She was glad to have a new client as she needed the money and business. With each new client, she could make a lot of gains developing her business through word of mouth, which was her best advertising. Yet she sensed there was more to this client. Only time would tell. Her imagination sometimes tended to work overtime. "Okay, Jackson." Bella gripped the phone, the weight of it pressing into her hand. "I can make time for you. Is next Wednesday at one p.m. suitable?"

"Of course. I'm pretty flexible with work. Thank you."

She hung up after giving him the address details and stared at the phone for a couple of minutes. She smiled to herself for having secured a new client. It could only get better. Within minutes, she picked up her desk phone. "Mari, can you open up my calendar and add Jackson's appointment for me."

"Of course. What's the date and time?" Bella was grateful to have Mari arrange her schedule on her online calendar. It gave her the time for more productive work. She was a godsend.

Chapter Six

A GRISLY SCENE

Detective Senior Constable Marco Petrazini stepped across rough, uneven ground strewn with stones, pebbles, dust, and rubble, making his way around the Brooklyn tip. He joined the officers already there and his partner, Tim, who was short, overweight and wearing a severe gaze. Marco assessed the scene before him. He grimaced at the rich smell of blood as he assessed the victim. "Hey, Tim. You've spoken to the officer on the scene?" He took out his notepad.

He nodded. "I have. The body was found at seven this morning by the manager of the site." He pointed. "He's over in the building, throwing up."

"We'll need to talk to him. Any witnesses or other staff present?"

"No, the other guy who works here starts in an hour. He was alone."

Marco knelt and bent down close to the naked body, careful not to touch it. That was the medical examiner's role. The woman's body and bone structure hinted at beauty, but her face had been disfigured with puncture wounds. He noted multiple stab wounds around the abdomen, some shallow and some deep. A small sentence had been carved into the top part of her chest, 'You've Been Marked.' *What did that even mean?* The body looked bruised and battered, with rope markings around her wrists. Her skin was grazed and cut around the ankles too.

Tim moved towards the body. "What are you thinking?"

He rose from his position. "This poor woman had obviously been tortured before being killed. A slow kill to prolong the killer's pleasure. Asserting their dominance over the victim with the stab wounds and the torture." He turned to an officer. "Let's cordon off this area and don't let anyone inside the perimeter. We'll need the ME to examine the body, and to contact Crime Scene. We also need to raise tarps to protect this area. If it rains, we'll lose whatever evidence there is." The officer nodded. "We need prints and an ID, and check missing persons cases, too. The torture was prolonged so I'm assuming she's been gone long enough for someone to miss her."

Marco took a few photos and a video of the body with his phone then interviewed other officers on scene. His partner, Tim, created a rough crime scene sketch.

"The perp has to be pretty strong to dump the body here. Probably used a van to transport the body."

"She definitely was dropped here like a piece of rubbish. Exposed and mutilated," said Marco. He grimaced and stroked his throat.

Crime Scene Unit eventually arrived, and Marco and Tim headed inside the building to interview the manager. The perp had used a secluded location with no visible witnesses, no security cameras, and no passing traffic. This killer was calculating. Marco made a note. Wind, debris, and dust most likely contaminated the scene, but they'd protected it as much as possible.

The interview with the manager proved fruitless. Nothing was revealed apart from what they already knew. They got the details of the other staff member and would interview him later to rule him out as a suspect.

Marco left the scene with Tim and stepped into the car. He sat in the passenger seat while his partner drove them to the police station. His heart wrenched at the thought of that poor girl's loved ones being delivered the bad news. Hopefully, they'd get an ID soon and could then notify the family. They wouldn't be able to claim the body until it was processed and examined for evidence.

Halfway through the ride, his phone buzzed. He picked it up, identifying the name on the screen. "Hi, Mum."

"Marco, I was ringing to see if you were coming over for dinner tonight."

He sighed. "I was about to call you, Mum. I think I'll be having a late night."

"Oh, Marco. You must eat. I will prepare something to fill your stomach, and when you get here, I'll warm it up for you. A man in your position must eat."

He shook his head, watching the half-smile on Tim's face. "Fine, Mum. I'll try to get there as soon as I can, but don't wait for me for dinner. Eat whenever you're hungry."

"Okay, and maybe one day you will surprise me by bringing a lady friend." He moved the phone away from his ear, his mother's screech almost busting his eardrum. "I mean, when are you going to give me grandchildren, Marco? When? I'm not getting any younger."

He ignored her. "Bye, Mum. I'll see you tonight." He hung up and turned to Tim, who chuckled as he drove.

"I think the next universe heard your mum shouting like a madwoman. She really wants to be a grandmother, Marco, so hurry up."

He put his phone into his side pocket. "She'll be waiting forever. Who has time for a relationship when we keep getting cases like this?"

"Part of the job being in the homicide squad," said Tim. "Besides, you like your women but you're afraid to commit. You love the thrill of the chase, a taste of different women, like a traditional yet typical Italian. Romance until it gets boring, right?"

Marco leaned back in his seat. "Hey, I'm only twenty-eight and was just promoted to detective, so I have my career to think about first."

"Sure, sure. Whatever!"

Marco swallowed, realising that he was definitely not ready for a serious relationship. He loved all kinds of women and treated them with the respect they deserved. They were a unique bunch with endearing qualities, and men would never be able to live without them.

Chapter Seven

ERROR IN JUDGEMENT

The following Wednesday, Bella held a notebook, her legs crossed, as she sat opposite her new client, Jackson. He had a blonde crew-cut, bright green eyes, and well-manicured hands. He appeared to be in his thirties.

They were already half-way through the session when she sensed he'd relaxed a little. She started to feel uncomfortable when his eyes trailed hers, and she had to break eye contact with him. His eyes scanned her from head to toe. It was as if he could see right through her. Many times, she had to look away or peer at the floor. She was frustrated with herself for feeling that way. She was a professional.

"I guess you can say that a friend of mine's been a great support with my anger."

"And your parents?"

Jackson squirmed in his chair. "I'd rather not talk about them, if you don't mind."

"That's fine, Jackson. Let's talk about the source of the anger, or when it started."

His lips set in a grim line. "Probably from my first relationship. I...I... guess. I got so angry that I pushed my fist into a wall. When she, aah, broke it off. I stopped myself from hitting her."

Bella continued to probe into his life and other relationships, trying to establish a pattern of type, but he had held back on a few things. This was natural for a first session.

"So, if I understand correctly, you feel the anger when your girlfriends decide to break up with you? Is that right?"

He nodded. "I guess that's it. I don't like it when they leave me. It hurts too much, and I don't know how to deal with my feelings then."

Bella nodded. "We can work on that in the sessions if you're open to it."

"I'd like that," he said.

"Tell me about your work. What do you do?"

"I'm an electrician by trade and run my own business."

Bella finished writing the last of her notes and shifted in her seat. Her shoulders ached, and a tension headache settled around the top of her head. They scheduled an appointment for the following week when they both rose from their seats. "I'll walk you out."

"Thanks." Jackson smiled and his eyes scanned her again from head to toe. The muscles in Bella's face tightened.

When she returned to her desk, she flipped open a page and wrote out her case notes. She assessed him as having Borderline Personality traits that had impacted his work, health, and relationships, but there was a greater mystery in his background. Did she really want to go there? Particularly with the way he had scanned her from head to toe, first in the beginning of the session and then at the end. He was definitely a charmer, but he wouldn't be charming Bella anytime soon.

Chapter Eight

TAUNTING

Climbing the few steps to the church and walking through the heavy red door on Saturday, Bella smelled incense mixed with women's perfume. She wondered why women who were learning Tai Chi would be wearing perfume when they'd be exerting themselves during the class. The atmosphere inside the church was fresh and noisy. She nodded to a few of the students then started her warm-up exercises.

As she was breathing in and out, eyes closed, she remembered that Claudia had failed to contact her within the scheduled few days. She was relieved that she would never work with Claudia again. She hadn't changed, and probably never would. There had to be more to it. Claudia normally had an ulterior motive to everything. She wore a mask that showed what others wanted from her, but in the end, she was never her true self.

Bella had seen that a few times while working with her. Once she had overheard her saying to another psychologist that all she really cared about was profits and not the clients. If she could string clients along and make them think they were still unwell, creating more vulnerability, the clients would keep coming back. Not only that, but she got too involved with her clients. It was a bit of a threat when clients felt overly exposed to someone who had a lot of power and could easily have them wrongfully institutionalised. Bella had wanted to report her to the Psychology Board, but she worried about Claudia's string of connections that could ruin her own career. She had had enough stress over the years, and she didn't need more of it. She could never win against a person like Claudia.

The instructor's greeting brought her back to the present. "Now, as we started last week, slowly bring out your right arm above your shoulder, keeping your posture straight, focusing on your breathing as your arm swings out to the side. Now do the same with your left arm. That's right. Keep the breath going, in and out, in and out."

Bella followed the instructor's lead, but her mind kept returning to Claudia and the dread that sat in her stomach. She pushed it aside and focused. She had another week left of Tai Chi and she wanted to make the most of it. Perhaps she would later continue with more advanced classes, or Karate that would teach her to defend herself. In the past, she never could defend herself, but it was important that she could now. Her sense of security was high on her list of priorities. The reason she became a psychologist in the first place was to help others fight against adversity and develop a sense of ongoing security.

Five minutes before the end of the lesson, Bella's phone rang. *Oh, shit!* She'd forgotten to put it on silent. She stopped her movement. "Sorry," she said to the instructor, who smiled. Retrieving her phone in her bag against the wall, Bella put it on silent. Claudia's number dominated the screen. She hadn't left a message, though. Bella quickly stuffed it back in her bag and returned to her spot.

At the end of class, Bella grabbed her bag and followed others towards the exit of the church. Her legs turned to lead when her phone vibrated against her hip. She popped her hand into her bag to get it and answered.

"Hello."

"Bella, it's Claudia here. Have you made a decision? Will you be joining me in the practice?"

Her feet froze to the spot as others around her ambled to their cars parked nearby or in streets surrounding the church. "I'm sorry, Claudia, but no thank you. I appreciate the offer, but I'm happy where I am."

"Are you sure? I mean, I'm only going to offer this once."

Bile rose in her throat. This wretched woman never gave up. "Yes, I'm sure. Thank you again."

"Fine then. Good luck with your practice. It's not easy getting clients, is it?" She didn't wait for a response. "Goodbye."

Bella put her phone away, her shoulders tense and her jaw clenched. *Don't let her get to you*, she counselled herself. A horrible thought occurred to her. Could Claudia manage to sabotage her practice? She wouldn't put it past the woman.

Rushing to her Corolla, she got a grip on herself, turned on the motor and drove off.

❦❦❦❦❦

After showering, meditating to relax herself after Claudia's call, and eating lunch, she booted up her laptop and checked her emails. Maybe she had further client enquiries.

Clicking on the emails, she was happy to see client enquiries and she responded to those. Several more emails down, a subject heading caught her eye. "BITCH!"

The hair on her arms stood on end. Curiosity won over the dread by a whisker, and she opened the email.

I guess it's been a week since my last email, so I thought I'd touch base. Oh, and by the way, I like the way you're learning Tai Chi. Preparing for a fight, or is it for stress? Good luck with that! You might need it in the future. I don't want you to get a false sense of security, but enjoy your life while you can. Just don't get too comfortable doing your Tai Chi. I'm always watching you.

Bella shook her head and tried to flex the numbness out of her fingers. This person was watching her and wanted to shake her security. Who was this, and why was she being targeted this way? Her training and experience taught her there wasn't enough information or enough of an overt threat here to take it to the police yet. She breathed in the golden light and exhaled the dark smoke. *I'm safe. I'm safe. My family can no longer hurt me.*

She needed to talk to her friends about this and get clarity.

Chapter Nine

A NATURE OUTING

The next day, Sunday, Bella walked alongside her friends, Jamie and Liz at the Williamstown Beach. Her feet stepped on the uneven surface of the concrete squares, feeling the salt-laden air brush her cheeks, and the sun searing her head. She focused on the double-story beach houses, the passersby going into the cafe across the beach, and Liz walking on top of the stone fence along the shore. Cawing seagulls surrounded her and settled on the mahogany wooden benches, then moved across to the hedge with its stone edging. Palm trees, canoes, and bike-stands lined the distance as the girls continued to walk along the beach, passing the kiosk and following the horizon.

"So, Bella, what did you want to talk about?" Liz asked as she stepped down from the stone fence.

Bella explained the two mystery emails that she was sure were from the same person.

"Oh, my God! Who do you think it is?"

Bella shrugged. "I wish I knew."

Jamie stared at her with concern. "Take those emails to the police, and make sure you never delete them. They might be able to trace where they came from."

"That's a great idea. You should do that," said Liz.

The girls turned back, took off their shoes, and stepped into the sand. Bella's feet sank into the soft damp sand and crushed shells. A couple walked their dog near the water. Bella loved the sound of the waves lapping against the shore. A shrill cry from a baby down the beach drew her attention to the families huddled in groups under umbrellas and inside tents. She wondered if those families took great care of their babies. Bella never got to see the beach as a child. She never got to go anywhere as relaxing as the beach. Her outings had been running errands for her family.

Boats drifted in the distant horizon and the red and yellow flags stood in the sand. A few girls sat on a towel and threw a ball around. The girls looked happy tossing that ball. Their family watched over them with loving gazes. One of the girls waved, and a woman she assumed was her mother, waved back. Her heart ached with longing. She yearned for her aunt and brother. Would she ever feel the simple joy of a loving family that others experienced growing up? She had had some great years with her aunt from eighteen, but as a child, it had been the complete opposite.

"Earth to Bella! Earth to Bella! Are you with us?" said Liz.

She turned to Liz. Behind her, Jamie placed a large towel on the sand. Both Liz and Bella joined her on the towel, metres away from the water.

"I'm sorry. What did you say?"

"Well, Jamie here is saying that you should go to the police, and I think she's right. It sounds serious."

Bella nodded. "I think you're right. I'll keep the emails as a record, but it could be a simple troll.

Jamie retrieved a bottle of sparkling water out of her beach bag. "I am not entirely sure that's the right thing to do, but it is your call, Bella."

Bella lifted her knees, her arms draped over them. "Maybe I'll wait and see if this continues, but I'll monitor the situation and not respond to it for now."

"You damn well better let us know if you get another message, Bella." Liz grabbed Bella's hand and gave her a reassuring smile. "We're with you all the way, but make sure you keep us in the loop. I know you're little Miss Independent, but we have your back, girl."

After talking the topic to death, Liz changed the subject. "And what are you doing about expanding your practice, Bella?"

"I've arranged for a book signing at the bookstore near the Port in town. I'll give you the details closer to the date. You and Jamie can come by if you're free."

Liz nodded. "Of course, we'll be there." She turned to Jamie.

"I'll reschedule things if I have to, but I will be there," Jamie added.

"I wonder if anyone will even buy my book."

Jamie sighed then took a sip of her water. She put the bottle back into her bag and fixed her gaze on her friend. "I have known you for about five years now, since your psychology internship at the hospital, and I have seen how much you have grown as a person in spite of your challenges. You simply need to believe in yourself a bit more and not let your father haunt you for the rest of your life. That belief will translate into your practice."

Bella chuckled as her face warmed. "I guess so, and such wise words. Thanks, Jamie. I am a work in progress."

Liz intervened. "Darling, girl. Jamie is right. You're great and special and deserve to have whatever life you want. Don't sell yourself short. Even when we did our degrees together, you sometimes let other people walk all over you because you didn't think you deserved anything else."

Bella rubbed the back of her neck and peered at the fine granules of sand. Her mouth was dry.

Grabbing a bottled water out of her bag, she took off the lid and drank. The silence between them was unnerving.

Liz grabbed her hand. "I'm sorry. We didn't mean to bombard you will all this, but we're your friends and we love you."

Jamie touched her gently on the shoulder. "We do love you, Bella. And, anytime you need to vent or cry, we are always here for you."

Bella fought back tears. She was stronger than this. "Thanks. Now, why don't we change the subject? How's your work going, Liz?"

"Great. Dealing with teenagers all day, who have been either emotionally abused, sexually abused, or physically abused sickens me on some days. Some of the stories you hear, are just horrific."

"You do have supervision, though, don't you Liz?" Jamie asked.

"I do, and she's great. My lifesaver, actually. Otherwise, you can easily burnout. I mean, with your job as a doctor, you can burn out, and Bella's work as a psychologist, she can burn out too. We're all health professionals so self-care's important. We can be accountable to each other."

Jamie nodded. "It certainly is important, but if we don't help these youths or children early, we will have a lot more criminals and possibly serial killers on our hands."

"Speaking of serial killers, I've been reading this great book by John Douglas called Mind Hunter. He was an FBI Profiler and talks about the mind of the criminal and how they're motivated to kill. It's really interesting," said Liz.

"I absolutely love that book. There's a movie based on that book too. It's on Netflix," said Bella. "I'm hanging out for season two."

"Fascinating," said Jamie.

Given what Bella had been through and her criminal father, she had almost chosen to study forensic psychology but didn't want to deal with the gore of murder.

Chapter Ten

DISCOVERY

Bella held her arms over her chest as she listened to Jackson's story about his ex-partner and her interfering father.

She shifted her posture as she fought back her own personal images. Everyone had issues, right? Even psychologists. She was strong enough to contain and compartmentalise her inner world and past torments, and that would be fine for now. If she went back down that road and opened up Pandora's Box, she didn't know if she'd be strong enough to live her day-to-day life.

"Anyway, enough about her. You asked me about previous counselling in the last session, and I remembered the psychologist's name. Her name was Claudia, and I saw her in Newport about a year ago, I think."

Bella winced. "You mentioned your previous psychologist was somewhat controlling. Was that who you were talking about?"

He nodded. "That's the one. I haven't seen anyone else."

"What else can you tell me about her?" She had to know about the boundary issues with her ex-employer.

His eyes rolled towards the ceiling as if an answer lay waiting up there. "She came to my house once, but I didn't let her in. I felt it was an intrusion on my privacy. I mean, she's not supposed to be giving house calls, is she?"

Typical of Claudia.

"You mentioned you were an only child. What was that like for you?"

He shrugged then stared. "Fine, I guess. I adapted."

"And tell me about your mother."

Jackson swallowed, turning away. He faced her again, presenting a wrinkled forehead and squinted eyes. He clenched his hands and sat more rigidly in his seat. "I'd rather not talk about my mother. Change the subject."

Bella nodded. She'd obviously touched a nerve. "Okay." She carried on with instances of anger with his latest girlfriend, and Jackson let down his guard slightly. "Are you able to sign this consent form so that I can speak to Claudia?"

His nose and forehead scrunched up. "Why do you need to speak to her? What good will it do?"

Bella sensed a density in the air, but she pushed through. "I normally speak to other professionals as a way to understand how I can be more helpful. You mentioned she was controlling. It's purely for the benefit of your therapy sessions, that's all, to know your likes and dislikes in therapy, and to work with you accordingly."

He nodded. "Fine. Hand the paper over."

Bella picked up the consent form and a pen and handed it to Jackson. He scrawled his name and signature with a darkness in his eyes. She picked it up and set it aside. "Thanks, Jackson. I will see you next week."

He rose abruptly. "Sure, whatever." He barged ahead as if he couldn't get out of there fast enough. What was it about speaking to Claudia that disturbed him?

Putting the thought aside, she checked her diary for Claudia's fax number then headed over to her fax machine. After sending the form, she called Claudia.

"Hello, Claudia speaking."

"It's Bella." She waited a few seconds for a response.

"Well, well, well. This is a surprise. Have you changed your mind about joining me?"

She held her knees and legs tightly together, her throat dry and uncomfortable. "No, nothing like that. It's a previous client of yours. Jackson Billiner. I've just sent you a fax. Do you have it?"

"Wait a sec." Bella waited for a minute while Claudia checked. "I just got your fax, and I got his case file in my archived section. I take it you want my perspective on this guy?"

"Yes."

"All I can say is that I saw him just over a year ago because of anger issues, but he never told me anything about his family. He's hiding a lot of stuff, but I couldn't figure out what. Then I went to his house once to get answers, but before you get on your damn high and mighty horse, I did it for a good purpose."

"And how did that go?"

"Well, he wouldn't let me in. He was a borderline psycho and shoved me. I couldn't report him because I broke my boundary as I do, but if you say anything, I will ruin you, Bella. Do you hear me? I will ruin you in more ways than one."

Bella stiffened. "I haven't said anything, and I won't."

"Anyway, I saw this woman in the background, but she had her back to me, so I didn't see her face. I heard her laughing as if she was enjoying the way he was throwing a tantrum in front of me. She might've been one of his victims of anger, but she looked fine and dandy then."

"Who was she?"

"He said she was a friend. He only came one more time after that and he apologised. But basically, other than his anger and relationship issues, all I knew about him was that he'd become possessive towards women, had absolutely no friends, and seemed to hate his parents. No siblings, according to him. Nothing more to tell you."

"Hmm," was all Bella said. "Thanks for your time."

"I take it you've just started seeing this guy for counselling?"

"Yes."

Claudia scoffed. "I hope you have better luck, but I doubt it."

Bella ignored the comment. "Anyway, I have to go."

She hung up and placed a hand on her chest, pondering. Jackson Billiner was a mystery, and she didn't know whether she'd get more out of him than Claudia did. What was he hiding?

Chapter Eleven

BOOK SIGNING

Bella passed the Hobson's Bay Yacht Club near the port of Williamstown, heaving the trolley of boxed books across the road, passing the church with its grey features, the set of apartments, and an Italian restaurant. A gentle wind rustled through the trees and the sunlight warmed her scalp. She fought off nerves as she pondered her desire to promote her book and services at this book launch. Sweaty hands caused her to lose grip on the trolley, so she wiped them on her top. Water for her parched throat would help ground her right now.

She was proud of her book. She'd managed to find time to write it, all about grief and loss, on weekends and evenings. Bella planned to write more books in the future, and having them self-published meant she could be flexible with her deadlines.

The bookstore was within her sights, and when she reached it, she lifted her trolley up onto the footpath, breathing heavily from the effort, and entered the shop. She smiled at the manager who towered over her with a bob style haircut and easygoing smile. She appeared to be in her fifties.

"Hello there, Bella. Welcome. I'm Judy." She extended her arm and shook Bella's hand. "Let me help you. Come through here." Judy pushed the trolley ahead and Bella

followed, squeezing her way through the aisles towards the back of the shop that had a little more space.

Judy set the trolley down. A long table had been set up, covered with a white cloth and a pile of bags for her to place the books into. "I've organised coffee in the staff room so customers can help themselves. I'll open the room now. Is there anything else you need, Bella?"

"No, thanks. I'm good."

Judy headed to the staff room and unlocked it while Bella opened the boxes and one by one laid out a few of her books in neat rows across the table. She had written about the theoretical aspects of grief and mental health, as well as outlining a few case studies and anecdotes. She hoped that by marketing her book, she'd get new clients to expand her practice.

Taking out a laminated book blurb with the title and price, she set it against a stand and placed it at the front of the table. Then she took out a plastic container for money storage and stationery items, setting them underneath the table out of sight, and sat to wait for customers. She took out a credit card machine and put it on the table.

People came in dribs and drabs and didn't stop by her table, preferring to browse in the store instead. As the store got busier with customers, she rubbed the back of her neck. *Calm down! Get yourself together!* Surely someone would come by her table to check out her book. Oh, sure they smiled at her, but no-one stopped by, and she wondered what she was doing wrong. This was her first ever book signing, and Liz had put pressure on her. She needed it not only to get her book out there but for her practice to survive too. She'd rather die than work for Claudia again.

Twenty minutes later, Liz and Jamie bounced towards her.

"Hey there, girl. How's it going?" asked Liz. "Any sales yet?"

Jamie snorted and shook her head. "Stop with the pressure, Liz." She turned to Bella and stood by her. "You look nervous. Are you okay?"

Bella shrugged, rising, and straightening one of her books so it lined up. She fiddled with the top button of her blouse. "It's only been half an hour. I'll be fine."

Liz clasped her hands together. "Do you want me to shout out to people and get them to come here?"

Bella laughed. "You are crazy, Liz, but no thanks. I'll be fine."

"I'm taking a few photos and posting them to Instagram. That'll get you more exposure," Liz said.

"Thanks. I was planning to take a few of the set table for Facebook. Just take a photo of the books on the table."

Liz frowned. "No, you need to be in it. You're the star of the show. Get yourself out of your shell, Bella. This is the only way that people will know you and your business. You have to take risks."

Jamie gave her a reassuring smile. "She is absolutely right. You need exposure if you'd like to expand the practice. Let her take that photo."

Hesitating, Bella finally said, "Fine."

Liz took out her mobile phone and snapped a few photos. "Do you mind if we browse and come back?"

"Of course. Go ahead."

Her friends walked through the aisles towards the front of the shop. Bella sat back down and squirmed in her seat as more and more people crowded past her. A few minutes later, a few people stopped by her table, and picked up her book and read the blurb.

"I'll take this. It sounds interesting," said a woman with grey hair and slight stubble on her chin.

"I'll sign it for you." Bella wrote a heart-warming message, signed it, took the money, and popped her book in a paper bag. "Thank you. I hope you enjoy it."

The other customers at her table left and went back to browsing. Bella suddenly stiffened in her seat. *What was Jackson Billiner doing here?*

Chapter Twelve

BROKEN BOUNDARY

Bella rose stiff-backed and shook her head, hoping that Jackson wouldn't notice her discomfort. He swaggered forward with a smile, wearing tight-fitting jeans and a t-shirt that said, "Men Rule."

"This is a surprise," Bella said, a sense of unease at seeing her client outside her practice.

Jackson shrugged. "Coincidence, I guess. I never expected you to be here."

She pressed her lips together and brushed a strand of hair out of her eyes. Liz and Jamie returned and stood by them, but they said nothing.

"Don't let me stop you from looking around." She wanted to say that she couldn't speak to him socially, but he was free to roam the bookstore.

He jutted his chin out. "Oh, sure. Of course, but I would like to support you. Never knew you'd written a book. Can I take a look?"

Bella nodded, spotting how the muscles in his face tightened. He gripped her book and clumsily flipped through the pages. She rocked back and forth on her heels, hoping that he'd leave her alone.

Liz leaned forward and whispered in her ear. "Who is that guy, and why are you sweating like the Amazon River?"

Bella said, "Don't worry about it. Did you find anything of value?"

Jamie neared her, showing her two books about anatomy and gut health. "I'm getting these. They look interesting. Have you had any sales yet?"

Bella nodded. "Just a few, but I'll be here for a few more hours."

Jamie beamed "All right. We'll head back home and speak to you soon."

Liz said, "I'll talk to you soon."

As they left, Jackson handed the book to her. "Can I buy this? It looks interesting. I think a friend of mine might like these ideas."

"Of course. It's fifteen dollars."

He handed her a twenty-dollar note but avoided her eyes. "I guess I'll see you in the next session. I'm looking forward to it."

She nodded, fighting back a wave of nausea, and handed him change. "Okay. See you then."

As he left, Bella sat back down and shook her head. She was never comfortable seeing clients outside her workplace.

The manager walked over to her side, getting her out of her reverie. "So how are things going? Do these patrons need a bit of a push?"

Bella smiled. "I've had a few sales, but I still have time for more."

The manager waved other customers over, but Bella's stomach tightened as she realised they were being forced to look over her book. The point of exposing herself this way was to do it all on her own. That was her way. She'd only had her aunt who had supported her throughout her young adult years. Her parents were a nightmare, particularly her father, and she wouldn't waste her energy on their pathetic lives. High school was another nightmare when she'd been alone, without the support of her parents.

After ten more sales, Bella packed up and thanked the manager. Her promotion had been reasonably successful, and a few people had expressed an interest in counselling. She had given them her card in the hope they'd ring and make an appointment.

Putting her boxes of books back on to the trolley, she waved to the manager and made her way outside into the warmth. With a resigned sigh, she pushed her trolley towards her car. She had the nagging feeling someone was watching her. She pushed the thought away when she reached her car and put the boxes into her boot. Her phone vibrated. She retrieved the phone from her bag slung over her shoulder and checked the text message that was short and to the point. She grew very still as she read the text.

I loved your book signing. There's no better way to get clients. Your time with me will come. She looked around wildly. This person was watching her! She didn't see anyone. Could they be in a car? Hiding behind something? Bella quickly loaded her vehicle and shut the door, hitting the locks. Her chest rose and fell with panic. Maybe it was time to talk to the police.

Bella parked under a tree close to a police car. She exited her own car and walked along an uneven, cracked footpath that led towards the flat-topped grey brick building with its row of rectangular windows. The police sign on the side of the building reflected the blues and whites painted on the doors. Two policemen stepped out of the building, expressions stern and serious, intimidating in their blue uniforms. She pushed back her panic and entered through the interior glass sliding doors, a sense of entrapment as she headed inside. Still pushing through her nervousness, Bella made her way to the counter.

An elderly policeman with a paunch and short, grey hair smiled. "How can I help you, Miss?"

She hesitated, hearing people coming up behind her. "I'd like to report a series of stalking incidences."

The policeman nodded. "Certainly." He pulled out a pad.

"Tell me exactly what's happened and when it all started."

Bella recounted the incidences involving the emails and text messages.

"Any known enemies or past boyfriends who might have a grudge against you?"

Bella shook her head. "Not that I know of at this point."

"And do you have a record of these messages on hand?"

"Yes, I printed out the emails and the text messages are on my phone."

The police officer took the copy of the email and a photo of the messages. "I'll hand these records over to an officer who can keep track of these, should you get further messages. We have a way of tracking your text and email messages, and what I would suggest is perhaps screen all your calls first. And I also suggest switching off the location feature on your phone. Limit your computer use as this can be tracked, particularly with social media. Furthermore, keep and date all items. Do not delete anything and advise us of further incidences. I have this discussion logged, so if someone else takes over, there's a record of your case. Take screenshots of anything untoward on social media and keep a record of any physical evidence or unwanted approaches or contact."

"Okay."

He forced a smile. "Keep in touch if anything further should occur. I've got a list here of where you can get more information about technology-facilitated abuse." He handed her a document.

Bella took it. "Thank you." She walked out with a slight sense of relief and a measure of control.

Chapter Thirteen

A TROLL

The cafe across the road from the Williamstown beach featured a cream weatherboard exterior and windows with a view of patrons. It was two days after Bella had made her complaint to the police. The beautiful October spring weather helped chase away the chilling notion that she was being stalked. Inside, the cafe with the smells of herbs, spices, and warm bread permeating the air, Bella, Liz, and Jamie walked inside. They sat at a square wooden table with ripped timber patterns and black plastic chairs. Sunlight streamed in from the side window. The front counter presented a glass cabinet filled with assorted cakes, bottles on a high shelf, and a television set high on a wall above the counter. On the table lay cutlery on a napkin, a sugar bowl, and salt and pepper shakers.

The girls rested back in their seats as a waiter approached and took their order. Liz ordered a chicken burger, Bella ordered a Caesar salad, and Jamie ordered a creamy risotto.

Liz fixed her gaze on Jamie and Bella and tilted her head. "I was wondering if you guys are free on the thirtieth of this month. I've been invited to this colleague's birthday party out in the Dandenong's."

Jamie shook her head. Her eyes drooped and black circles nestled underneath them. She was always working too hard, and Bella wondered how much sleep she had last night. "I can't. My parents are having a charity event and they're forcing me to go. Sorry."

Jamie turned to Bella. "What about you, Bella?"

A sick feeling filled her stomach and she held her breath for a moment. "No, I can't go."

Liz knit her brows and crossed her arms. "Do you have something on, or you just don't want to go?"

Bella hesitated when the waiter brought their food. *Saved by the food!* The girls dug into their dishes after the waiter left. A baby howled in the distance, and a family sitting behind them laughed at a joke.

"Bella?" said Liz.

"I'm sorry. You know I hate parties."

Jamie smiled at Bella reassuringly then brought her drink up to her lips. She took a sip and set the glass down. "Leave her alone."

Liz blushed. "That's only because she hardly ever goes out with us." She turned to Bella. "It's as if you turn into a pumpkin at night. I mean, I've known you for about nine years, girl, and in the past year since your aunt died, I can't even count on one hand the number of times we went to parties or nightclubs. I know your aunt was important to you, Bella, but she'd want you to move forward. Wouldn't she?"

"Slow it down a notch, Liz," said Jamie.

Bella was dumbstruck, her mind tuning out. She didn't know what to say or how to make Liz understand. It was sometimes too hard to face her grief and her past, especially when triggered. "I'm sorry, Liz, but I'm just not ready to face huge crowds. Please understand that I still need time."

Liz bit her lip. "But what better way to learn than to face your fears? You know that better than anyone, as a psychologist."

"I know that, but I can't this time. Please, Liz. Don't pressure me." She forked a lettuce leaf into her mouth and crunched on it. "Next time I'll make the effort, okay."

Liz let out a huff of frustration then went quiet. She dug into her remaining burger and licked her fingers. She wiped her mouth as drips of mayonnaise oozed down her lips.

Jamie looked up after eating her risotto. "Listen, I have a story about one of my colleagues. Her name is Martha, and she's having a hard time because her husband's been unfaithful. She hates him now and has moved out of the house. She's staying with me for a few days until she decides what to do."

Bella adored Jamie for changing the subject. She always seemed to know when Bella needed rescuing. "That's terrible. Must be a shock if it's his first time cheating." She ignored the knots in her stomach.

"It is the first time, but he claims to love this new woman. She is in shock. Any strategies I can use, Bella?"

"All you can do is listen and be there for her. Offering her your home is a grand gesture. She might need time apart from him to decide what to do next. Has she met the woman?"

Jamie shook her head. "Not at all. I don't think she would want to either. What do you think, Liz?"

Liz shrugged. "It sucks, but what can you do. I've had boyfriends cheat on me before, which is why I prefer to be single now. I guess you get those cheating types and those monogamous types. It's in the blood, you know."

"I hope she will be okay. In spite of hating him, she still loves him. I've met him and he is one of those arrogant and overconfident types. I don't know whether she'd be able to sort things out, especially if he claims to love this other woman," Jamie said.

Bella said, "If the relationship is new, it'll soon get old, and he'll probably realise it was only lust. Might give him time to reflect on things. He'll get into a routine with his new girlfriend, but that routine will probably make him realise that whoever he's with, the adventure doesn't last."

"At least there are no children involved," Jamie added.

Bella nodded. Her phone vibrated, but she ignored it and finished her meal. Her phone vibrated again, and again, and again.

"Someone's in a hurry to get to you," said Jamie. "Aren't you going to check that?"

"I will in a minute, but I want to apologise." She lay a hand on Liz's. "I'm sorry, Liz. I promise you I will come to the next party. You can hold me to that."

Liz warmed. "I know, and it's okay. Maybe one day you'll make me understand why you can't let go. I know there's a lot in your family history, but you have to let us in. We're your family now."

Bella fought back tears and dug into the last of her salad. In spite of her strong response about not going to the party, the guilt settled in the pit of her stomach. She hated hurting her friends this way, and she hoped that next time she'd feel differently.

When Bella's phone vibrated again, she retrieved it from her bag and clicked on the screen that brought up her social media account. This account advertised her private practice, and now she'd received a comment on social media that related to her practice. Her body went cold as she gripped the phone.

Bella Carismo has no soul, no honour, and only cares about taking your money. She will ultimately take over your life. This so-called therapist needs to lose her licence. Do NOT trust her. Ever!!

Jamie leaned forward. "What is it? You look spooked."

Liz moved closer and read her screen. "What the hell! Who is this loser?"

"Can someone please kindly tell me what the problem is," Jamie said.

Bella handed her the phone and Jamie read it. She stared up at her friend. A prickling of her scalp and quiver in her stomach kept her frozen. Her goal to expand her practice was ruined on social media. "This is coming from Claudia's Facebook account."

Chapter Fourteen

LASTING BONDS

Bella held a rigid posture. "I'll go pay. I need to get out of here."

Jamie rose. "No, I'll pay this time. You and Liz can go to the park, and I will meet you there."

Liz nodded. "Come on, let's go. It looks like you're suffocating in here."

Bella smiled without joy. Her chest felt tight. "Thanks, Jamie."

Bella and Liz headed out towards the park, their strides aligned as they crossed the road. Dry, dead leaves crunched beneath her feet, and the clouds were slowly turning darker as if rain was imminent. The fresh smells of the trees and seawater did little to calm her nerves as she kept up pace with Liz once they reached the picnic areas. Jamie caught up.

The perching seagulls around them were fluttering, and the low wind rustling through the trees was sporadic. Sounds of children playing on the playground with parents watching and chuckling. Happy families. Something she'd never had as a child made her feel more alone than ever. In spite of having her friends, Bella missed the family she'd lost. She thought about her brother and aunt.

Liz took her hand, jolting Bella back to the present. "Hey, girl. Are you okay?"

She shrugged and fought back tears. "I'll be fine."

"Listen, nobody's going to listen to that stupid post. People who know you in the counselling world will know it's a sham. Do you really think it's Claudia?" said Liz.

Bella turned towards her. "The question is whether the account's fake or not. She thinks that she has every reason to ruin me because she can't control me, but I don't know."

"Anybody can hack into anyone's account. Easy peasy nowadays. Or they can create fake accounts. You know how many fake accounts have to be closed down every day?" said Liz, who looked out into the distance.

The usually comforting breeze against Bella's bare neck felt harsh against her skin. The sun's rays made her squint. Greying clouds rolled in, their shade foreboding. "Probably lots. Anyway, Claudia hates me because I initially threatened to go to the board because of what she was doing. She hates me more now because I refused to work with her again. What better way to get me to work at her practice by ruining my reputation? She's always been manipulative, Liz, and I'm sick of her controlling my life. Not only was I attacked by that patient because he thought I was like her, but she bullied me out of that place. I can't go back there."

Liz frowned. "And you won't have to. Your practice will survive this. The important thing is that you don't respond to trolls. That's all they are. Trolls. I mean, it could be someone jealous of your new counselling practice who knows that you're good at what you do. Don't let them get to you, girl."

Bella nodded. "You're right, as usual. Thanks."

Jamie put an arm around Bella's shoulder. "The right clientele will come to you. Stay strong!"

"I don't know. I'm just wondering whether it really is Claudia doing this to me."

Jamie shifted from one foot to another, watching the children in front of them. "Wait and see how this pans out, but I would suggest you advertise your services as per normal and ignore the post."

"That's exactly what I plan to do. Ignore it."

Liz tightened her bag strap and cleared her throat. She fidgeted and bit her lower lip. With a nervous breath, she said, "You don't think this person is the same one that's been sending you those other messages?"

Bella's mind was on Claudia. "I don't know. I still think it might be Claudia."

Jamie's eyes peered at the ground. "And would Claudia have the capacity to stalk you this way?"

Bella sighed. "She might, but I don't know. Why now? Why would she do this to me now when I haven't worked with her for a while?"

"I guess that's the million-dollar question," said Liz. "Anyway, let's change the subject. On to brighter things." Liz looked into the distance. "Over there, Jamie, there's this cute guy who seems exactly like your type. The academic sort with the corporate outfit and the regal air. I wonder what he's doing here dressed up for business."

Jamie pursed her lips. "I have no time for a relationship, Liz. You know that I am not only focused on my work, but I have my book club, my work experience students to mentor, my occasional fund-raising activities, and my gym activities. I suppose if I don't sleep, I could have the time for a relationship." She shook her head. "Anyway, I don't see you in a relationship."

Liz's eyes turned dark for a brief moment. "I'm enjoying single life, and partying, and going to the gym more often now too. It's less complicated without a relationship." She stared off into the distance and seemed miles away. Poor Liz had had a bad relationship that had turned her off men. Bella had become friends with Liz at university while studying for a Bachelor of Arts Degree, but when Bella went off to specialise in psychology, Liz specialised in social work.

Bella intervened. "Maybe I'll go after that guy myself. If I try the corporate type rather than the usual casual, romantic type, I might have better luck with men."

Jamie chuckled. "And you deserve to be happy, with your own family." Her eyes turned serious. "I am so glad you chose to do your psychology internship at the hospital. Otherwise, you and I would never have met."

"I'm glad too, Jamie," said Bella. She fought back tears.

Liz leaned towards them both, wrapping her arms around them. "I say family hug all round." All three friends huddled in a group hug bringing tears to Bella's eyes. This was her family now and she knew they had her back.

Chapter Fifteen

DISTURBING NEWS

Bella unlocked the door to her office a few days later. Footsteps and a car door closing got her attention. She turned around, knitting her brows as she watched a man getting out of a dark SUV and heading towards her. He was of average height, with short brown hair and stubble on his chin. He wore a leather jacket over tight-fitting shirt and jeans that showed his well-toned, muscled physique. As he got closer, she could tell his eyes were hazel and he had a sweet, handsome face. A short, stocky man with a bald patch walked alongside him.

The man stopped before her and held out his hand to shake hers. "Hello, I'm Detective Senior Constable Marco Petrazini from the local police department." He flashed her his badge. "And this is Detective Senior Constable Tim Wittens. We'd like to ask you a few questions about a Miss Bridget Mardot. I understand you were friends with her back in high school?"

Bella froze on the spot, her mind taking her back to the worst days of her life. "Sure, I knew her. Has something happened, Detective?"

"Can we come in?"

She nodded. "Of course. I don't have a client for the next half hour." She turned back to the door and swung it open. She led the detectives to her office and they sat down. Bella sat in her desk chair, facing the detective. She had a bad feeling about this. Her hands started shaking and her throat dried up. "Can I get you a coffee or water?"

He shook his head. "No, I'm fine. I'd rather get into it, if you don't mind?"

"Okay. What's this about?"

He cleared his throat. "I'm sorry to have to tell you this, but your old friend, Bridget Mardot, was found murdered a few days ago."

Her shoulders slumped. Bella turned to the jug of water on her desk. She poured water into her glass with a shaky hand, spilling some of the liquid on her desk. She wiped it away with a tissue, downed the water, and turned back to the detective. A bead of sweat rose on her upper lip. She remembered being stood up by the woman.

"What happened?"

The detective fixed his gaze on Bella. "She was tortured and stabbed twenty-seven times."

Bella placed a hand over her mouth, tears pouring down her cheeks. "Oh my God. Who would do such a thing?"

"That's why I need to ask you a few questions. I understand you had telephone contact with Bridget a few weeks ago. Her mother said you called her after being stood up, and that was when I assumed she'd been missing...until we found her."

Bella reeled at the news, cringing. She took another sip of water, letting the liquid soothe her dry throat. "That's true. I haven't seen Bridget since high school. I was sixteen when my family moved closer to the city, and that was the last time I'd seen her."

"What did she say exactly when she called you on the phone?"

She took a deep breath. "She was different on the phone, not like the way I remembered her. She sounded almost civil, not like when I knew her back in school, which was hard for me to believe. She basically said she wanted to make amends for bullying me in high school. I didn't answer her right away but then agreed to the meeting later. I thought maybe I could get something out of it too, even though I had mixed feelings about the contact. Then we arranged a date and time, and she hung up."

"Do you believe she was genuine about wanting to make amends?" asked Detective Tim.

Bella shrugged. "I didn't really believe her, to be honest. It sounded almost forced, like it was scripted."

"And nothing else was said?" The detective asked.

"No, it was a quick call. Very strange, though, how it just came up out of the blue."

Bella now wondered if Bridget had had something important to tell her, but now she'd never know the real motive behind the proposed meeting. Did she truly want to make amends? And why now, after all these years. Something must've happened for her to want to fix things between them.

He nodded. "Can you tell me anything about Bridget back in high school? What she was like, and who her other friends were."

Bella's hands started to sweat. Her heart rate shot up. She closed her eyes briefly, an image flashing before her eyes. She was back in high school.

Bridget pushed Bella's face down into the toilet bowl, shrieks of laughter resounding behind her. "I should let you drown in this water. You deserve it, bitch!"

Bella's face submerged in the water, choking and gasping for air. She pulled her head back out, barely able to breathe. She coughed and took deep breaths. She couldn't make out the blurry figures around her. Bridget and her friends chuckled until

Bridget stretched out her leg and kicked Bella in the stomach hard. Bella clasped her arms around her stomach, cowering and shivering. She swallowed and rested against the cold, damp wall of the cubicle, tears pouring down her cheeks. Her friend, Dawn, entered the bathroom a few minutes later, wrapping her arms around her, stroking her hair and cheeks. Without a need for words, Dawn walked her home.

Bella brought herself back to the present, her hands visibly shaking. She looked up at the detective who stared with inquisitive eyes. He didn't need to know everything about her past. She didn't know how she'd feel talking about it all, either.

"Ms Carismo? Are you okay?"

She nodded, refusing to give him the whole sordid details. "She was a bully, but as bad as she was, I am not a killer, detective. I am not built that way."

"I'm not accusing you of anything, Ms Carismo." He fixed his gaze on her. "Did she bully others?"

"Plenty of kids at the school, so take your pick."

"We are questioning her current family and friends."

Bella's chest tightened. "I didn't like Bridget, but she didn't deserve to die. No-one does."

Detective Marco nodded. "I may have further questions. I will be in touch." He rose and saw himself out.

"Thank you for your time," said his partner.

Bella rested back in her chair, fighting off the images that came in torrents. She had to get ready for her next appointment. It was useless and unhelpful to dredge up the past again.

Chapter Sixteen

CRIME REFLECTION

Marco ambled out of the building and adjusted the collar of his shirt. He fanned his face against the heat in his cheeks, but it wasn't terribly hot outside, just mild. Maybe it was from the heat in the building.

As he and Tim stepped into the car, Marco's mind flashed back to Bella. Her silky, shoulder-length brown hair, soulful bright green almond-shaped eyes, and those dimples on her cheeks as she attempted a smile before he gave her the bad news. Something in her eyes was sad, yet sweet and innocent. There had been a fleeting look of sadness, but she hid it well when she spoke to him. It was like she kept up a pretence for the sake of interacting with other people.

He wondered what her real story was, and whether Bridget had truly wanted to make things right. No matter how much of a bully Bridget was, she didn't deserve to die that way.

When they arrived at the police station, they headed to their respective desks. Marco sat down in his swivel chair and ignored the scurrying feet of the other detectives who were on the phone, milling about, or huddling over cases in the open plan desk space. He grabbed a manila folder from underneath the clutter of thick case files and flicked it open. Staring at the naked body of Bridget, he flinched at the twenty-seven stab wounds. What was the significance of that number? And why such rage towards her? So far, they'd talked to her mother who hadn't offered anything about current enemies. They'd also interviewed friends who had mixed feelings towards her, mentioning how she was fun to be with but could also be self-absorbed and selfish. If that was the case, then he doubted that she had really wanted to resolve things with Bella. She must've had another reason to request the meeting with her, but what was it?

The few acquaintances they'd interviewed mentioned how Bridget had bullied a few people at school, but no-one had shown any rage towards her. At least not to the point of torturing her or engaging in overkill.

He put the photo away and dug into the medical examiner's report. The perpetrator had restrained Bridget's legs in stirrups, tied her up securely with a rope, stabbed her, creating superficial and deep wounds, crushed the bones in her upper body with a sledgehammer, and cut out her tongue. The killer no longer wanted her using her words. *Quite a sick puppy we have here, but why now? What was the current trigger?*

Bridget also had tranquiliser in her system. *So that must've been the way the killer incapacitated her.* Put her out, took her to a kill zone, then dumped her body at the tip.

His telephone rang. Checking the caller ID, he cringed at the name on his screen. *Violetta!* He didn't want to ignore her, so he answered the call. "Hey there. It's been a while."

"Hey, Marco. I've been busy." Violetta was his ex-girlfriend. They had broken up a few months ago, but they had remained friends. In spite of breaking up, they had decided to have an arrangement when they occasionally got together for intimacy. "I was just wondering if you wanted to have fun tonight."

Marco's arms and shoulders tensed. He glanced around the station uneasily and replied in a slow, yet gentle manner. "I wish I could, but I'm busy on this new case."

"Not a problem. If you're busy tonight, what about next Friday?"

Marco hesitated. An image of Bella popped up in his mind. *What the hell?* He never had thoughts about the civilians on his cases. "I'm sorry. I'll be held up for a while. Maybe I'll call you in the next few weeks."

"Oh, cut the bullshit, Marco. If you no longer wanna be friends with benefits, then just spit it out. I've had enough of men feeding me lies just to save face or spare my feelings. I'm a big girl. I'll survive."

He admired her feisty nature, but it was also the reason they were no longer dating. "Fine, Violetta. I'm sorry, but this won't work for me. I wish you well, but you deserve someone who isn't me."

"Not a problem, cutie. Take care."

Marco's hands became fists as he stared at his phone. He was far too busy to focus on bootie calls.

Chapter Seventeen

CHANCE MEETING

Bella and Liz met in the hospital cafe during Jamie's break from the emergency ward. The cafe buzzed with visitors. The hard-backed chairs, the queue to ordering food a mile long, the smells of greasy fat, and the patter of feet walking to and from the counter gave Bella a headache. She stared at her sandwich, not having an appetite as she pondered her old nemesis, Bridget. The way Bridget was attacked was deeply personal and filled with rage. It had to be someone close to her or someone who had vengeance on their mind. Bridget must've suffered horribly. Bella stopped her thoughts and refused to think of that horror now. There was nothing she could do about it. Had she studied criminology instead of psychology, she'd have a better understanding of the motive behind the death. Yet, she harboured no regrets in her choice or profession, as profiling horrific deaths would eventually have impacted her.

"Penny for your thoughts," said Liz.

Bella looked up, pressing her lips hard together. "Sorry, I'm not feeling that great today. You can have my sandwich."

Jamie bit into her salmon roll then delicately wiped her mouth with a napkin. She put down her roll and clasped her hands. "Now, you both came here to have lunch with me, so you need to eat. I know the issue with your friend is disturbing, but from what you told me about her, she was not a very pleasant person."

Bella swallowed. "She wasn't. I'm just wondering who could do such a thing. I mean, that many stab wounds. Not your normal, everyday killer. It was deeply personal, and I guess it's put the fear in me. My troll is nothing compared to this."

"Speaking of your troll," Liz said. "I think you need to confront Claudia, call her out on this. It's most likely her after what you told us. Right? You lost a few clients over this."

Bella sighed. "What's the point? It won't fix anything. Without taking a chance on me they chose to notice that stupid message on Facebook."

"All the more reason you need to speak to Claudia and get her to stop," Liz said.

Bella shrugged. "And what if it's not Claudia? You said it yourself that it might be a fake account. I don't know for sure that it's her."

Liz leaned forward and held on to her chicken schnitzel and salad roll. "How do you know unless you confront her? I'm sure you'll be able to tell if she's lying or not."

"I don't know," said Bella. "She'll most likely deny it, even if it is her."

Jamie unclasped her hands and fixed her gaze on Liz. "Let Bella make her own decisions. She is old enough to decide what is best." She looked behind her when someone called out her name. "Oh, it's Martha."

A towering woman with strawberry-blonde hair, an attractive face, and a stocky figure ambled to their table. Her puffy eyes were red, as if she'd been crying and her shoulders drooped. "I'm sorry to disturb you with your friends, Jamie. Do you have a minute? It won't take long."

Jamie looked apologetically towards the others. "Of course, Martha." She rose and headed outside the cafe with her colleague.

Bella wondered what else had happened with Martha. A new development in her relationship, perhaps? Or maybe she'd met the husband's mistress? If they could have counselling, they might have a chance to work things out, but the trust had to be rebuilt.

Bella took a bite of her salad sandwich when Jamie returned. "Is everything okay?"

Jamie shook her head. "Martha found out that her husband's moving in with his girlfriend, so he told her she could move back into their home. She's taken the rest of the day off so wanted my house key to start packing up her things. She is devastated, poor thing."

Liz frowned. "I guess that means there's a slim chance of them working it out?"

Jamie nodded. "Probably, but she still holds on to hope."

Bella lay down her sandwich. "Would you like me to talk to her?"

Jamie smiled. "Let's see how this pans out, but maybe she will consider counselling later when it all sinks in."

"Not really counselling. I don't expect her to pay me but just a bit of support and understanding."

"That is generous of you, Bella. I can ask when I see her next. I might visit her tonight and make sure she is okay." Jamie rose and sipped the last remnants of her juice. "I'm sorry ladies, but I better get back to the emergency ward. As a doctor, these poor patients cannot wait for me forever." She rushed off with a wave.

Bella stood up next. "I have a client at one-thirty. My only one for today, after all these cancellations I've been getting. Thanks to social media."

Liz rose and followed Bella outside the cafe. "I'm sorry, but I am spreading the word about you."

"Thanks, Liz but I've applied with Employee Assistance providers, so I should get some work with them if they don't follow my social media."

"You haven't had more posts, have you?"

"No, and, hopefully, it doesn't continue. I did report it to Facebook Admin though."

"That's good. Anyway, my car's over there. I'll talk to you soon, love," Liz said.

Bella waved goodbye and walked a few metres towards her car. The sun suddenly went down as the grey clouds started hovering. The fresh, crisp air made her body shake slightly. As she approached her vehicle, she unlocked her car door. A tug on her shoulder made her gasp. "Don't scare me like that, Liz..." She turned around. Jackson's eyes peered straight into her own. He smiled and stood so close she could smell a whiff of his cologne. It was musky and strong.

"Well, hello there, Bella. We seem to be bumping into each other a lot. What are you doing here?"

Bella had nowhere to go so she moved back and leaned against her car, feeling the cold metal against her back. She twisted the hem of her t-shirt and avoided his eyes. "I had lunch with friends. What are you doing around here?"

He hesitated. "Ah, just caught up with one of the managers here about an electrical contract for work, that's all."

She wondered if he was telling the truth. "I have to go. Sorry."

He drew in closer and bit his lower lip. "What's your rush? Don't you have time for a quick drink or something?"

Bella cleared her throat. "I'm your psychologist, Jackson and there are rules about this. Boundaries. I really need to go."

He rubbed the back of his neck and his face tightened. "Explain the boundaries to me."

Bella's face warmed and she looked at him briefly. She would stand her ground and not let him intimidate her. She could do this. She'd managed far worse than this in the past. Straightening her posture, she said, "As your psychologist, I can lose my licence by going out with you in any capacity. Our relationship is strictly professional."

He crossed his arms. "Fine. I guess I don't want you losing your licence. That would be tragic. You are a great psychologist, after all." He smiled. "I'll see you at the next appointment then."

Bella waited for him to move back. He finally took a step backward. She entered her car, and with a shaky hand started the motor. In the rear-view mirror, she could see Jackson standing on the road, watching her.

What was going on with this guy? He was starting to push boundaries with her. The best thing to do was to stop sessions with him. She'd break it to him gently at his next appointment.

Chapter Eighteen

AMBIGUOUS VISIT

Walking through the door of the small concrete building, feigning confidence, Bella approached the buxom receptionist at Claudia's private clinic in Newport. "Hi, Jenny. I'd like to see Claudia."

The receptionist smiled. "Hey, Bella. It's good to see you again."

"You too," Bella said.

"I heard you started your own practice. How's it going?"

"Slowly. Getting a few regular clients, but it's still new."

"Well, good luck." She beamed again. "I'll get Claudia for you. Take a seat."

"Thanks."

Bella turned back and sat in the waiting area where several people sat near her on black and white chaise lounges. She noticed a few changes in the waiting area since she'd worked in the practice. A huge television screen stood out above a large fish tank containing a group of tropical fish, and a glass coffee table featured an array of women's and men's magazines. The flooring was white plush carpet with off-white walls featuring paintings of landscapes, abstracts, and prints that displayed a range of affirmations below the designs. The ambience was relaxing. Soothing jazz music played in the background. Claudia definitely catered to the higher-class and must've been doing well with her business judging by the improvements. Could Bella ever do this well in her practice? At the rate she was going, she might have to close it down and forget about working with people if she was going to be taunted at every turn.

Maybe she could have music at her practice too and upgrade her furniture if she ever got a few more steady clients.

Shifting her posture, Bella looked at her watch. Four o'clock. She'd finished with her last client at 2:30 p.m. and had a small client load again tomorrow. If she continued at this rate, she'd need to start looking for another job. She shook her head. No, she had always been able to take care of herself and would never resort to living a life she didn't want.

Claudia came out into the waiting area sporting stilettos, a dark fitted cotton jacket over a white silk blouse, and a tight black skirt. She looked every bit the professional, even if she broke boundaries with her clients. She gazed at Bella briefly with a curt nod and whispered to a burly man. "Sorry, John. I have an urgent meeting that shouldn't take long. Do you mind giving me ten minutes? We can add the time over to your next session."

The man nodded. "That's fine, Claudia."

She smiled at the man then approached Bella. "Come on through."

Bella rose and followed Claudia through a narrow walkway. She turned into a medium-sized office with a large desk topped with manila folders, stationery, and thick books. "Thanks for seeing me. I won't be long."

Claudia looked at her sternly, her lips pressed tightly together. She didn't invite her to sit. They both stood awkwardly near the desk. "What do you want, Bella? I have a busy day and I'm one staff member down."

She retrieved her phone and clicked on the old post. Handing it to Claudia, she said, "I'm just wondering if you wrote this."

Claudia's eyes scanned the screen. She tilted her head and turned away for a moment. "I never wrote this, and I am appalled that you think I did."

"But it came from your account."

She scoffed. "Anyone can hack into an account. I am sure even you know that."

Why did she need to be patronising all the time? She took a calming breath. "I am sorry that I turned down your offer but I'm happy where I am."

Claudia chuckled. "Are you trying to imply that I'm getting back at you with this post?"

Bella shrugged. "I didn't say that, but I guess I am wondering who would do this to me."

"Hmm, maybe you're not the high and mighty psychologist you think you are."

Bella drew a hand through her hair then massaged her wrist. "But this person talks about boundaries."

Claudia squinted. "Well, you thought wrong. I wouldn't waste my energy writing something like this. Maybe you need to face the fact that some clients don't like you. It has to be a client."

Bella started to rise. "So you haven't sent me strange texts either?"

She flinched, then peered at her watch and rose. "Like I said, I wouldn't waste my time. Now if you don't mind, I have a busy day, and obviously you don't. You can show yourself to the door."

Bella fought back the urge to slap her. She walked towards the waiting area and watched Claudia as she strutted towards her male client. Bella couldn't tell if Claudia was lying or not, but she was manipulative and wouldn't put it past her. There wasn't anything Bella could do if she didn't have any proof.

Chapter Nineteen

AGGRESSIVE NATURE

Bella played with the tips of her fingers, peering at her watch every few minutes. Her queasy stomach stopped her from reviewing last session's case notes of Jackson. She intuitively knew that Jackson was hiding many things about his life, but the question was why did he feel the need to be secretive? Did he have something shameful to hide?

Bella wondered how many of the tools and strategies she provided he was applying, and whether he wanted to deal with his issues. He appeared to show great insight into his behaviour, but something held him back. A wall that she'd probably never break down. If a client didn't have the willingness to face the issues at hand, no amount of skill by any psychologist could change that.

She suspected he was attracted to her, which was why she had to stop treating him. After supervision with her mentor, Bella was surer than ever and knew that this was the right thing to do. In spite of needing clients, she couldn't compromise her ethics and the law, given the boundary Jackson had crossed.

Her phone jolted her into the moment. Bella picked it up. "Yes, Mari?"

"Jackson is waiting to see you."

"Thanks, Mari." She hung up and took a calming breath, placing a hand across her chest. Releasing all the tension in her body, Bella closed her eyes and let out an audible sigh. She strolled out to the waiting area and peered at Jackson. He was sitting with one leg over his knee and his hands clasped in his lap. He wore fashionable attire of a crisp white shirt, a black suede jacket, and black cargo pants, obviously doing well in his electrical contractor business.

"Hi Jackson. Come on through." The hair on the nape of her neck stood out as he stared right through her as if sensing all her deep, dark secrets. It was disconcerting.

He followed her to her office and Bella almost lost her footing as she sat on her chair.

"Are you all right there?"

"Of course." She smoothed the top of her skirt while holding a pen and notepad.

After providing another spiel about boundaries, Bella discussed referring him on to another psychologist. She winced at the way he looked right through her again and his hands clenched into fists. "I'm sorry, Jackson, but this isn't going to work. I can refer you to another psychologist in the area. I won't charge you for today, but I wanted to let you know that I don't work with people who cross boundaries."

He leaned forward, smirking. "Is this because I asked you out? No big deal. If I can forget about that, then so can you. Water under the bridge."

"It is a big deal." She avoided his eyes, uneasy in the way his eyes dug into her own. "I feel you'd be better suited to a different psychologist. I've given you some strategies to help, but in effect, they're mainly bandaids and nothing more. You might feel more comfortable opening up to someone else to look into deeper issues."

He chuckled. "I guess you want to hear how my mother had sex with her boyfriends in front of me? How she went crazy after my father killed himself? Or when I got shuffled from one foster carer to another because my mother passed out from alcohol almost every night? And how I initially made my living? Oh, there's more but I won't go on." He stopped and turned away.

Bella fought back nausea and pushed down her emotions. She angled her head, curious. "I'm sorry to hear that, Jackson." She fixed her gaze on him. "How did you make a living at first?"

He shrugged. "Nothing. Just forget it."

She wondered whether there was hope for him yet, but what he'd recounted sounded horrific. He seemed genuine about it, and his body language stiffened as he offered those unthinkable actions by his parents. Maybe it was an act to gain sympathy, thinking that would change her mind about continuing therapy. No matter what, it was not possible to continue working with him.

Her mind flashed back to the hospital the other day and how he got too cosy with her. She couldn't ignore that and doing so would be going against her professional ethics. As soon as anyone got too close to a client, it was time to break off the therapeutic relationship.

"I'm sorry, Jackson, but I really can't help you as the lines have been crossed. We'll have to say goodbye."

His face paled as he shook his head. "No, I'll open up. I promise. I will. Just give us a chance to work through this. We've only had about six or seven sessions. Please, don't do this to me. I really need help."

Bella looked down into her lap and swallowed. "I can't do this, Jackson. I'm sorry. You'll need to leave now."

Jackson closed his eyes and when he opened them again, he wasn't looking at her. His eye twitched and his head shook. He rubbed his hands together. Quite unexpectedly, he charged towards Bella and grabbed her by the wrists. He pushed her back against the chair. "You bitch! You bitch! You can't do this to me. I never trusted you anyway. You're all the same."

Bella pushed against him, trying to free her hands. "Jackson. Stop this. It's Bella. Please look at me." His right arm stretched out as he slapped her hard across the cheek. She fell back and hit the back of her head against the desk. She rubbed her head and felt a slight bump, but she pushed herself back up. Jackson pushed her back down and she lay on her back as he sat on her stomach. He spat in her face. One punch against her eye triggered the anger in Bella. She struck a blow to his own cheek, and he fell back on his side when she kicked him in the groin.

"You filthy cow!" He towered over her and was about to hit her again. Bella reached up with her arm, and for the second time, slapped him hard across his face. He twisted away and quickly moved off her, his body shaking. He pressed both hands against the side of his head, frozen in place. He seemed to have awoken from his fugue state, zombie-like, still frozen in place.

She headed for the door at the same moment it burst open. Mari rushed in. "Bella, Bella. Are you okay?"

"Call the police and lock this door."

Bella closed the door and waited for Mari to retrieve the key as she closed Jackson in. She quickly locked it with Jackson inside. "And please get rid of the client in the foyer. Reschedule them."

Mari said, "Of course."

Bella closed her eyes, her heart racing. The old images flashed before her.

She blanked out for a second and stared up at the obese man with missing teeth. Her father! He ripped open her t-shirt and pressed a cigarette butt to her chest. "This will teach you not to answer me back." She screamed and passed out yet again.

Mari returned and grabbed her hand, pushing her towards the waiting area. "Sit on the couch and tell me all about it." She stroked Bella's hand and looked over towards her office door with a shake of the head. "That creep. I should've known he was bad news the first day he walked in here. I had this funny feeling about him."

"It's okay. I'll be fine."

Bella wondered if she'd really ever be fine again, as it wasn't the first time she'd been attacked in her office.

Chapter Twenty

INCIDENT REPORT

Bella shook when Detective Marco handed her a glass of water from the filter jug in the waiting area. She drank it down quickly. He had brought in police officers who had arrested and charged Jackson with assault. They had taken Bella's and Mari's statements. The look on Jackson's face as he walked out of her office was twisted. Initially, he was cold and icy, as if he wanted to kill her with his eyes, then his eyes had softened. She shuddered thinking about his words, "I never trusted you anyway. You're all the same." If only she had referred him on to someone else to begin with. If only Claudia had warned her about his real persona. Not that she ever expected anything from the woman.

The detective unbuttoned the top part of his crumpled white shirt, showing a tanned neck, a few chest hairs, and taut muscles. He wore tight-grey pants and Italian leather shoes, as immaculately dressed as he was the first time she had met him. His eyes fixed on hers as he watched her gather herself. He sat across from her at her desk and held a notebook in his hand as if he wanted to ask further questions.

Bella swallowed. She looked up at him, her face flushing. Images of her father flashed before her as she fought hard to push them back into the recesses of her mind. She refused to go there. Too hard. Too much. She could only deal with her present right now, and the detective had curiosity in his eyes.

"Are you okay, Bella? Do you need me to drive you home?"

Bella shook her head and crossed one leg over another while pushing down the end of her knee-length skirt. "I'm fine, Detective. Is there more that you need to ask about Jackson?"

"No, but we'll question him and make sure he doesn't come back here. The police medical officers might have a chat with him, seeing that you mentioned he was in a dissociative-type state. They can determine if he's mentally unstable." He gripped the notebook. "Are you okay for me to ask you about Bridget?"

Bella's chest tightened. "Sure, that's fine."

"Or we can do this another time."

She almost lost her nerve, but she needed the distraction from Jackson, as grim as that distraction was. "It's fine, detective. Go ahead."

"I'd like to ask you more about who else Bridget might've taunted back then. A person's history can determine a lot about someone's present life."

Bella took herself back to high school, recalling how Bridget would bring extra clothes to school, dress up, and apply the brightest red lipstick she had ever seen. She had wondered who Bridget was meeting but she never knew who the boy was. Bridget would turn to her before leaving to meet him and say, "I doubt you'll ever find anyone to love, Bella. Who'd want to love you?" It wasn't the first time she had heard those words.

She returned to the present. "Bridget had one boyfriend after another, so you might need to interview quite a few boys from her last year in school. I'd gone to a different school for the last two years of high school. I can give you a couple of names, and not because she told me, but the rumours were rife around the school." She jotted them down on a sticky note and handed it to him.

Marco rose. "Thanks for that. We'll look into it. I'll let you know about Jackson, and if you remember anything else about your school days, no matter how trivial you think it is, just give me a call." He handed her a card and when their hands touched,

Bella's chest surged with heat. She put it down to the possible malfunctioning of her air conditioning system.

Bella walked to the nearby park to catch her breath after today's incident. She sat on a bench, the air smelling of fresh green ferns and scented flowers. The sunlit sky soothed her skin as she lifted her face to warm it. The darkness of the sky soon settled over the suburb, grey clouds shifting past. Closing her eyes, Bella brushed her fingers along a locket her aunt had given her a few months before she died. Bella hardly took it off. It had always brought her comfort whenever she'd been shaken to the core.

Her phone vibrated in her bag. She opened her eyes and rummaged into it to retrieve her phone. She clicked on the screen and words in capital letters stood out. Her heart almost got caught in her throat.

Reading the text, she froze at the words, *"Liz is in an abandoned warehouse at this address in Carlton. Be there in forty minutes or she dies."*

Bella blinked several times before the words registered in her head. This had to be a joke. She dialled Liz's phone number. No answer! Then a shiver told her not to treat it as a joke. How in hell could she get close to the city in peak-hour traffic in forty minutes?

Chapter Twenty-One

COMING TO LIFE

Sitting at his office, Marco drew a hand through his hair and stared into his lap. He couldn't get the tortured image of Bella out of his mind. That bastard Jackson really did a number on her, but she'd kept it together even though her eyes betrayed her. Those emerald-green eyes haunted him, troubled him, as if she'd been through so much in life. He had the feeling that more than Jackson's attack impacted her deeply, but what? He wondered where her mind travelled to as he had handed her the glass of water. When their hands had brushed against each other after giving her his card, his chest had tingled. She was beautiful on the inside and out, but he couldn't think of her that way. It was wrong, and Marco liked the freedom to see different women whenever he had the need. He loved all women, so why settle for one? Besides, it would be bad for his career to get involved with someone who was connected to a case.

A slap across his back alerted him to the present. He looked to his side and Tim squinted towards him. "Where's your head at?"

He shrugged. "Nowhere." He lifted his head and fiddled with the mouse at his computer. "I was just taking a look at Bridget's Facebook page, the more recent posts. Diabolical." Tim pulled over a chair and sat beside him while Marco clicked on a post featuring a pose where she bent over and demonstrated a g-string she was wearing. Another post showed her kissing two different women.

"She's been busy," said Tim.

"Hmm," said Marco. Let's watch this video, dated a couple of weeks before her murder." He pressed play.

"Hey guys and gals, I'm here to officially invite you to a very private reunion at my house. I want all my high school buddies and old acquaintances to come so we can celebrate our ten-year reunion. Now, I know that some of you might not want to come, and that I might've been a bit of a bully back then, but I assure you that I was immature in high school and have grown up a lot in ten years. I want us to all be friends and put the past in the past. Now, check out the deets below this video, and I'll see y'all. Oh, and don't forget that I'm promoting a new swimwear range. Love ya!"

Tim frowned. "What do you make of that, Marco?"

"Fake as anything and superficial. She hasn't changed in this video. She still craves attention and wants the power to influence people. A hidden agenda to make her famous, but I question the real reason she wanted to meet Bella."

Tim shifted in his seat. "Maybe she needed her for something. I know that Bella's written a book, so maybe she thought Bella could make her famous or something. She obviously craves public attention."

"I don't know. I mean, after all these years, why contact her just before the reunion when she would've been busy organising that? Unless she wanted to convince Bella to go to the reunion for whatever her agenda was."

Marco scrolled down to other posts and cringed at the provocative pictures and poses. A few of the poses featured her revealing her cleavage and kissing a few different men. She was inclined both ways, and obviously enjoyed fun. Maybe too much fun. "Damn shame the place she was murdered is too isolated for witnesses. But I have a hunch that the possible trigger for the murder was this school reunion."

Tim fished gum from his pocket and chewed. "So, you're thinking it's someone she might've bullied back in the day?"

"It's possible, but it's also likely she might've upset someone in her current life. She's had a chequered lifestyle with one boyfriend after the next. Maybe a jealous boyfriend."

"Or a jealous girlfriend," said Tim.

Marco cleared his throat and turned away from the computer. "Were there any matches with the tyre tracks?"

"Nope, nothing. No visible footprints either. We know that it wasn't a sexual crime as she wasn't sexually abused, so are you thinking a hate crime?"

"It's likely, given the way she's presented herself." He turned back to the screen. "We need to interview these friends of hers and rule them out. Possibly a huge waste of time, but even one of them might offer us a lead."

"Sure. Who do you want to see first?"

"Her latest boyfriend then we'll look at this girl she kissed."

Marco grabbed his jacket from behind the chair and headed out with Tim, wondering whether any of her friends would torture her in such a vile way. Only time would tell.

Chapter Twenty-Two

TIME RUNNING OUT

Bella raced out of the park after reading the address, knowing roughly where the warehouse was located. She ran as fast as she could towards her car. Her legs felt like jelly and her heart almost leapt out of her chest. *Liz! Have to help Liz.*

At the sight of her car, she dug her keys out of her pocket. They slipped out of her hands. *Damn!!* Quickly, she bent down to pick them up off the ground. *This had to be a joke*! Fishing out her mobile phone, she dialled Liz's number again. It went straight to voicemail. She tried Jamie, but no answer. *Oh, no!*

A quick click on the remote and the car came to life. She jumped inside and sped towards her destination. She drove over the speed limit as she zigzagged around slow cars and vans. An accident up ahead slowed her down. *No, no!* She had to find a quicker way. She racked her brain for other roads with less congestion. If Liz died on her watch, she would never forgive herself. She would rather die if it came between the two of them. Why was her stalker targeting Liz? For control or to send her a statement that Bella needed to pay for something? Who was this person?

A car horn jolted her out of her reverie as she realised she had cut someone off and was very close to clipping them on the side. There had to be another way. Now she was bumper to bumper with other cars. She would never make it to the warehouse in time, so she detoured on to another road. Another ring on her phone signalled a text message. Slowing down, she retrieved the phone and skimmed through the message. *"You have twenty-five minutes left. You've been warned!"*

"Oh my God! I've already lost fifteen minutes in this damn traffic! I have to get there in time. I have to, no matter what." In the back of her mind, she hoped this was a sick joke. It had to be. If this went pear-shaped, she'd hate herself.

She pressed her foot hard on the pedal and increased her speed, her hands sweating on the steering wheel. Her chest constricted and her head weighed her down. A truck up ahead slowed her down again. Bella overtook the truck and narrowly missed another car in the oncoming lane. She almost didn't care whether she lived or died. At least she'd die trying to save her friend, but she couldn't die. Not now. Not when she had the chance to save Liz.

Bella reached Flemington Road, but the lights were killing her. She had saved a bit of time taking the shortcut but now she'd lose time in the city congestion. Her breathing erratic, she dialled Liz's number again, but there was no response.

Taking a calming breath, she eventually sped past the Royal Children's Hospital and the Peter MacCallum Cancer Centre until reaching the large roundabout. Waiting for the lights to change was excruciating. She looked at the dashboard clock. She still had at least ten minutes. Not far now.

Finally, the lights turned green, and she pushed ahead, almost tail-ending the car in front of her. *Not long now. Not long! Hang on, Liz. I'm coming.*

Slowing down along Cardigan Street, Bella searched for the number of the building until she'd found it. Quickly parking the car on the kerb, she rushed out and double-checked the numbers. This was the number the person had given her, but where was the abandoned warehouse? It was a cafe, a familiar one.

Bella ran inside the cafe and a man with a moustache smiled behind the counter. Out of breath, she asked, "Excuse me, but I'm looking for a warehouse around here. Is there one close by?"

The man looked at her strangely, his head tilting. "No, love, sorry. No warehouse around here. Are you looking for someone?"

She shrugged. "Never mind." *This was a sick joke.*

Quickly, she texted the person messaging her back. She waited five minutes but no reply. Bella called Liz again and again. Finally, a response. "Hello, Liz. Are you okay"?

"Bella, hi. Of course, I'm okay. What's wrong?"

She breathed a sigh of relief. "Are you at work?"

"Yes, I'm at work. Where else would I be?"

She took a relieving breath and placed a hand over her heart, the rhythm slowing down. "Nothing, never mind. I called you a couple of times, but you didn't answer."

"I was in a couple of interviews, but I'm finished now."

Taking another calming breath, Bella said, "I'll talk to you later."

"Bella, wait. What's going on?"

"Nothing. I can't get into it now. I have to do something."

"Okay, I'll call you later."

Bella hung up and closed her eyes briefly. This was an obvious wild goose-chase that her stalker probably laughed about. Liz was never in trouble. She was fine. This address led her to a cafe. She'd been there before, years earlier.

She heard a ding and checked her phone. Swallowing and reading through the text, her body froze. It was from her stalker. *"Oops, sorry, but someone won't be so lucky the next time around."*

Bella flexed her fingers and arm muscles and clenched her teeth. She wanted to hurt this bastard so badly she wanted to scream. How dare he do this to her! Scurrying around the area, she peered in the distance and up close, near the car parking area and inside cars. A man was staring into his mobile phone, but as she got closer, he was face-timing a woman and together they laughed. She ran towards the park and looked behind trees and bushes, near other cafes, but no-one around her looked suspicious. The bastard had to be close by, watching her. He had to be here, and she wanted so desperately to find him. What was this stalker playing at, and why was she being targeted?

Pulling at her hair, she bowed down and clutched her hands to her chest, her heart beating fast. As it slowed, she closed her eyes and absorbed the sun flaming her cheeks and the wind grounding her. She wouldn't let this bastard get to her without a damn fight. And that was a promise to herself.

Chapter Twenty-Three

ANXIETY

Bella awoke the next morning, stretching out her arms and yawning. The sun's glare caught her eyes and she squinted. She forgot to close her blinds last night. Sitting up in bed, she leaned back against the bed head. An uneasy feeling settled over her as she replayed the text message from yesterday over and over in her mind. The dread, the fear, the sick feeling in her stomach made her want to vomit all over again. She sensed that things would get worse before they got better.

This bastard was playing games with her, gaining control without any regard for human emotion. What had she done to cause this kind of hatred in her stalker? She was reliving her childhood all over again.

The wild goose-chase could've caused a car accident because of the crazy way she was driving. She could've killed herself or others. Liz didn't pick up her phone a few times and this led to her thinking of the worst possible outcome. She wondered why the stalker got Liz involved, but most likely to taunt her and get back at her by choosing her friend. She only hoped that Jamie wouldn't be targeted next. She had to speak to the police about this new development.

Bella got out of bed, the cold surface of the floorboards waking her up further. She headed into the kitchen, put coffee and sugar into a mug, then watched the steam rise from the kettle as she poured water into the mug. Not feeling hungry for breakfast, she sat down, sipped her coffee, and wondered again who could be hurting her this way.

Her mind turned to Bridget. If she were still alive, she'd be the type of person who would taunt and bully her like this. She'd bullied other girls, too, but Bella must've caught the worst of it because she had defended someone. Bridget didn't like anyone going against her.

Bella showered and dressed. Another quiet day at the office with only three clients seeing her today. Another two clients had ceased sessions, but she had spoken to new doctors further out of Williamstown and was hoping to get referrals. She had secured one of those new clients today. Her old school had also contacted her about speaking to the students about bullying, given the school had their share when she attended. Apparently, they had a new principal who was making new ground in the fight against bullying. She had agreed to the talk, but it wasn't for a few months.

Bella thought about her old friends from high school. She had lost touch with most of them. She had managed to get away from Bridget in Year 11 and made a new group of friends in her final two years at a different school. Intermittently, she had kept in contact with two of her old friends from her subsequent school.

She opened her door, walked out of the house, and locked it behind her. A tap on her shoulder made her jump. Turning around, Liz grabbed her hands.

"Sorry, girl. Didn't mean to scare you, but we need to talk."

Bella sighed. "Hi Liz, but I have to get to work. Can we talk later?"

Liz shook her head and pulled her closer to the fence. "You worried me yesterday, and I know that something's going on. What is it?"

Bella hated to burden those she loved, but Liz was feisty and persistent and would never let up. It was either be hounded by her all day and night or give it to her straight. She did have a right to know, but why worry her?

Bella placed a hand on the low picket fence and gripped tightly. Liz stood with her hands across her waist, waiting. Eventually, she explained the text message she'd received and the stated threat on Liz's life.

Liz drew back and briefly turned away. "You've got to be kidding. No way would this stalker go this far. Hell, how dangerous is this person, Bella? I'm really starting to panic here. Playing jokes and causing you unneeded anxiety. Who the hell is this prick?"

Bella shrugged. "I don't know."

"We need to go to the police with this and I'm coming with you. Do you have time now? I can reschedule a couple of things at work today and go in later."

Bella nodded. "Okay, let's go and talk to the police. I have a bit of time before my first appointment later this morning. I was going in early to do paperwork, but that can wait."

Chapter Twenty-Four

NEW INSIGHT

Bella and Liz waited at the police station to speak to Marco. She had first asked for whichever officer was handling her case, but he wasn't available, so she asked for the only officer she knew. Marco. Butterflies formed in Bella's stomach as she thought about the stalker's escalation. She hadn't been hurt physically, but emotionally she was a mess. It was beginning to affect not only her sleep but her work too. Ruminations kept her up at night and she found herself drifting off while clients told her their story since this all started.

A masculine voice made her turn. "Hello, ladies." He nodded. "Come on through." Bella and Liz followed the detective down a narrow walkway and into an open-plan area with a cluttered desk space.

"Take a seat." The detective sat behind a desk while Bella and Liz sat across from him. He looked at them quizzically after taking out a notepad and pen from a side drawer.

His desk sported a pile of in-trays with stacked documents and books. The detective scooped up manila folders with case files and inserted them into a drawer beside him. A towering bookshelf behind the desk held books covering profiling, serial killers, and police procedures and statutes. Landscape paintings filled the wall above the desk, and newspaper articles featuring commendations and awards he'd received for solving crimes stood out.

"What brings you by, ladies?"

Liz turned to Bella. "I think you should explain what happened yesterday."

Bella nodded, aware of the detective's fixed gaze. Her nerves made her stomach tingle. She gave him the details of her statement to the officer when she was initially stalked. He clicked on a few buttons on the computer and squinted at the screen.

"Yes, I can see your statement here. So has something else happened, Ms Carismo?"

She nodded. "You can call me Bella." His face softened. "Yesterday, I received a series of text messages threatening Liz, telling me that if I didn't reach her in forty minutes, she'd be dead." Bella went on to explain her actions and all the texts she'd received from her stalker. The detective's gaze didn't leave her face once while recounting the story, and she found herself fumbling with her words.

He clasped his hands together. "Liz, have you ever responded to any of those messages, either on the phone or on social media?"

Liz shook her head. "No, I only offered Bella advice, but nothing more. I don't know why I'd be targeted."

"Most likely because you're close to Bella. It's a way of hurting her deeply when those she cares about get hurt. In this case, it seems it was only a threat, but I'd like you both to take precautions."

He fixated on Bella. "I assume the initial officer gave you the necessary information about stalking."

"He did," Bella said.

"Let me take a look at your phone so we can check it out. Have you blocked that number?" She rummaged into her bag and gave him the phone.

"No, I didn't. I thought it might be useful for the police."

"I assume you've stopped contact on social media."

His strong gaze made Bella's heart race. "I closed my account and I have a security alarm at home. My neighbour keeps an eye on things at my house too."

The detective gave her a reassuring smile. "That's good. Just keep a record of everything. We can look into things a bit deeper." He faced Liz. "Sorry, but I need to speak to Bella privately. Would you mind waiting outside? I won't be long."

Liz shook her head. "Not a problem, detective. I'll wait outside."

The subject of his discussion changed. "I was meaning to call you about your former client, Jackson. The police medical officers determined a history of trauma and dissociation. Are you still wanting to press charges?"

Bella winced. He wasn't himself at the time, and so long as she had nothing to do with him, he'd stay away from her. "No, that's fine, detective. If he comes after me again, I'll get an intervention order against him."

She wondered about Bridget. "Any new leads on Bridget's murder?"

Marco rubbed his hands together. "Nothing I can share at this stage, but we're still digging deep."

"I hope you find the killer."

Marco smiled, his gaze travelling down to her lips. "I hope so too. Anyway, I'd be happy to check in on you from time to time, given this stalker situation. I want to make sure you're okay. Stalkers tend to escalate, and I'd like you to be extra careful."

"That's fine, detective. I'll get going now." Bella drew a hand nervously through her hair.

He rose from the desk and stretched out his hand to shake Bella's. The lingering touch of his hand caused shivers down her legs. "I'll be in touch." He let go of her hand and gave her an awkward grin.

Bella rose and headed to the exit. Once she reached the car outside, Liz turned to her. "Oh, my God, Bella! He's got it bad for you, and you for him."

Bella's stomach leapt. "What?"

Liz chuckled. "He has the hots for you. I mean, the way he kept looking at you and how tenderly he touched your hand. Oh, he really likes you."

Bella's face warmed. She shook her head and swallowed. "That's crazy! He's just a nice guy and being polite."

As they walked to their respective cars, Liz said, "Hmm."

Bella's mind kept flashing to Marco's penetrating gaze, his gentle hazel eyes, his toned body, and thick lips that made her wonder how they would feel. No, this was madness! She couldn't think about him that way. He was way out of her league. Besides, she didn't need the complications of a relationship right now.

Chapter Twenty-Five

MEETING WITH HER NEMESIS

A few days later, Bella got a phone call from Claudia to meet with her for coffee at the Nelson Place cafe. It was a quiet Saturday morning as she walked along the empty street. She loved Melbourne's first seaport which was scenic for tourists and locals alike. Nelson Place featured tree-lined parks, museums with a World War II ship and a range of retail stores, cafes, and restaurants all nestled to form a popular marine village.

The fresh sea air and the waterfront restaurants with its historical buildings gave Bella a sense of warmth and calm when she enjoyed a casual meal or experienced fine dining with her friends. It was the perfect place to let loose and set aside her worries for the day, particularly when she was able to frequent bookstores, art and craft stores, and the local craft market.

Lingering in her steps and almost reaching the cafe, she heard something close by. Footsteps sounded behind her. Turning around, there was no-one in sight. She stuck her hands in the pockets of her jeans and peered at the ground as she walked. She rolled her shoulders to try and release the tension there. *Just relax. You're on a public street. You're almost at the cafe. Nothing bad is going to happen to you.* She heard footsteps again. When turning back around, she spotted a young couple kissing as they strolled. She was being ridiculous and paranoid. Bella laughed at herself. She was still on edge after the incident involving Liz and today hadn't been off to a great start.

She had frantically searched the house for her aunt's necklace but couldn't find it anywhere. She was certain that she'd placed it in her jewellery box, but it was nowhere to be found. With a heavy heart, she walked out of the house without it, hoping to search again later today.

Grounding herself, she entered the cafe. Bella scanned the room until she noticed Claudia waving her over. With unsteady steps, she forced a smile and sat across from her, a glass of wine in Claudia's hand. She displayed immaculately ruby-polished nails and wore a tight-fitted blouse, a skirt, and gold hoop earrings. Bella didn't want to be here, but at the last moment, she had no excuse in mind.

Her eyes roamed the cafe, which was dimly lit, quiet, and smelled of spices. Customers slowly strolled into the cafe, but it remained quiet.

"I am glad you came." Claudia avoided her eyes. Obviously, her words were insincere.

Bella lay down her bag and clutched her wrists with both hands. "Why did you want to meet?"

"I am sure you know that this is about Jackson. I mean, how in heavens could you cease counselling when the poor man has abandonment issues?"

Claudia had no right to berate her like this. How typical of her. "How did you know?"

She clenched a hand and stared at her nails, looking bored. "He came to me and explained the misunderstanding, and said he wanted to see one of my psychologists."

Bella wanted to laugh. Was that what he called his aggression? A misunderstanding. "He attacked me, Claudia. How would you have responded?"

"Gee, I don't know, but maybe try to de-escalate the situation?"

Bella wanted to wring her neck. Who in hell did she think she was after the way she had broken multiple boundaries with her clients? "I tried, but he had some kind of flashback. I couldn't bring him back to the present. He dissociated. Whatever it had made him violent and I had to protect myself and my staff."

The waiter arrived and took their orders of a latte for Bella and an espresso for Claudia.

Claudia pressed her lips together and crossed her arms. She smiled a hard, tight smile. "He asked for a medical report about his trauma history. He said something about possibly needing it in the future."

"I'm dropping the charges against him, but if he comes back to my practice, I'll be contacting the police again."

Claudia changed the subject. "Jesus, woman. He has only asked for a report. I don't think he plans on doing you in. Whatever's going on with him, the report will be genuine and written by one of my psychologists after a thorough assessment. If you don't want to work with him, we will." She paused. "Anyway, have you had any further social media situations? I do hope you've stopped blaming me."

Bella shook her head. "No, I haven't had anything more on social media."

"Great." She fidgeted with her hands. "So anyway, about Jackson. I don't think he'll bother you again. We are happy to take him off your hands. After the assessment, he can have therapy and group sessions if he so chooses."

Bella jerked her head back. "After what happened last time, I wouldn't think he'd come back to you after the assessment."

Claudia chuckled. "Oh, Bella, dear. Have I not taught you anything? The man has money, and I can seriously make a lot of money out of him. I plan to run anger management programs, and that will definitely be another source of income. He needs us."

The waiter arrived with their drinks, and he left with a smile and a nod.

Bella wanted to wipe that smug look off Claudia's face, but she fought back her emotions, choosing to remain detached. She added sugar to her drink and stirred it, taking a sip. "But he's dangerous, Claudia. If he flashes back again, he can attack you. He's paranoid and doesn't trust people."

Claudia smirked. "I have a different relationship with Jackson, and I know how to control him. Don't you worry your pretty little head, Bella. I've got this." She waved a hand in dismissal. "I wanted to do the right thing and let you know what I'm planning. You can still join me in the practice. After all, isn't your practice in dire need of clients?"

Bella clenched her fingers and took a calming breath. "I have clients, thank you, Claudia. I also have speaking engagements. Besides, Jackson will not come back to you."

"If you say so."

Oh, what she would give to give Claudia a true piece of her mind. This woman took any opportunity to put her down and make her feel like rubbish, but no more. She wouldn't let her affect her this way. She had to put a stop to it.

After finishing their drinks, Claudia rose from the table and grabbed her bag. A hint of gold stood out. It was a gold chain. She looked further inside her bag and cringed. Her necklace! What was it doing in Claudia's bag?

Claudia fingered the piece of jewellery. She paused and looked at it for a moment, then placed it back inside her bag.

Bella stood close to Claudia. "That's my necklace. What are you doing with it? I lost it this morning."

Claudia's mouth fell open and she gasped. "Yours? Are you serious?"

Bella nodded. "Yes, I'm serious. Can I please have it back?"

Her hand flew to her chest as she gave Bella an incredulous stare. "I was... ah... ah... going to hand it in to the police. It's not mine, after all."

"I don't think you were. How did my necklace get in your bag? I had it at home. You were trying to steal it, weren't you?"

"Don't be ridiculous." She fished the necklace out of her bag. "Here you go. Have it and leave."

Bella grabbed the jewellery and stormed out of the cafe. As she was walking to her car, she almost tripped but regained her composure. How did Claudia get her necklace?

Chapter Twenty-Six

AFTERNOON TEATIME

After the meeting with Claudia, Bella parked her car outside her house. She sat in her car a moment, pondering how on earth the necklace had ended up in Claudia's bag. She had appeared nonchalant about the necklace and had surely lied about wanting to hand it in to the police. Any normal person would've acted surprised and mention to their companion how on earth a strange necklace would appear in her bag. But there had been none of that.

Bella brushed aside the thought and stepped outside. She spotted her neighbour, Beatrice, who was pruning roses in the front of her colonial-style home. Her rose bush flailed in the wind and with the force of Beatrice's pruning, her eyes focused intently on it until Bella walked by.

"Perfect spring weather for pruning roses," Bella said.

Beatrice looked up and gave a gloved wave. She put down her shears and stepped over leaves, dirt, gardening tools, and weeds to make a beeline for Bella. She took off her glove and prodded Bella towards her home. "Come on in, dear. You look a little worse for wear. A nice cup of tea will make you feel better." She took off the other glove and threw it behind her. "Besides, I could do with a break."

Bella nodded. "Sure, I'd like that. Thank you."

She followed Beatrice inside the house, a pungent smell of cat pee and cigarettes in the air. The narrow foyer led to the small-sized kitchen with a few pots and pans lying in the sink. More dishes lay stacked on a rack.

Bella sat at the round table while Beatrice turned on the electric kettle. She took out two mugs and prepared her brew of tea. She poured the boiling water into the mugs and set one down in front of Bella, placing hers opposite. Beatrice opened up a packet of Tim Tams and lay them on a tray. She placed the biscuits in the middle of the table. "Anyway, have a biscuit, Bella. I didn't have time to make my own."

"Thank you. These are my favourite."

Beatrice took a sip of her tea then joined her hands together, her grey fringe covering the top part of her eye. She flicked it back and smiled. "So, tell me, dear, what's been on your mind?"

Bella had known Beatrice for the past year, and she felt a connection to the woman who enjoyed her company. She'd been a comfort to her after her aunt died and was like the grandmother she never had. It was refreshing to have an older person nurture and care for her the way her parents should've cared for her.

"Oh, it's nothing really. Just some problems at work that should hopefully sort themselves out." She refused to worry the poor woman by telling her about Jackson or her stalker. The woman didn't deserve to hear her troubles, not now and not ever.

"That's good. I'd be happy to listen if you'd like to share."

Bella clenched her hands, fighting to contain her words. "Like I said, it's all good. How are you doing with your health?"

Beatrice sighed. "Trying times, but I manage. My daughters come around when they can. They're busy with their own children so I can't burden them too much. I have my pride after all."

Bella nodded. "I have seen them come by a few times, and they always seem to be rushing around with your grandchildren."

"Those grandkids certainly keep me on my toes, and I wouldn't have it any other way." She turned her gaze past Bella for a moment then watched her again. "You know, I noticed a couple of days ago a woman hanging around your house. She rang your doorbell and when you didn't answer, she peered through your windows as if she was curious about something. As if she needed to get inside the house, looking rather flustered."

Bella leaned forward, curious. "What did this woman look like?"

Beatrice placed a finger over her lips, turning away for a moment. "She looked a bit older than you, but smallish in build with light-coloured hair tied up in a bun."

That sounded like Claudia. What the hell was she doing at her house? What was she even looking for? It might that have been the time Claudia had taken her necklace from her bedroom? But how did she get inside? Maybe she had a way of getting into people's homes without a key. "Did she say anything to you, Beatrice?"

"No, nothing dear. After that, she got back into her car and drove off."

Bella put the matter behind her. It was probably nothing. They discussed Beatrice's holiday plans with her daughters, and how she needed to save up enough money for the trip.

"Tell me about your family. I don't think I've ever seen your parents around. Do they live far from here?"

Bella cringed, twisting her shirt-sleeve anxiously. She leaned back in the chair and avoided her neighbour's eyes. "They live far from here, so I don't see them."

"I imagine you visit them from time to time."

She shook her head, chewing on a fingernail then swallowed. "Not really, no."

Beatrice's eyes darkened. "I've never asked you about your parents before because I sensed that something wasn't quite right. I am here to listen, Bella, if you'd like to talk."

Bella leaned forward and squeezed her hand. She'd be forever grateful to this woman for bringing a bit of light into her life. Over the years, she'd had a dark and sombre kind of life, but maybe one day, that would change. "Let's just say that my parents aren't very nice people. At least my father wasn't. My mother was fine some of the time. I don't see them at all."

Beatrice knit her brows and pursed her lips. "How long has it been?"

"Oh, about ten years." She hoped the woman would change the subject, not wanting to hurt her feelings by telling Beatrice to stop talking about her parents. Although she often wondered whether her parents ever had any regrets or remorse. She greatly doubted that and hoped to never bring them up with Beatrice again. It was a waste of energy.

Chapter Twenty-Seven

VANDALISM

Early Monday morning, the late October sunlight, soft and warm against Bella's cheek put a smile on her face as she took a short stroll in the park before work. The first intense rays of the day, a symbol of summer to come in the month after next. Looking up at the sky at the few white puffy clouds that created flowing patterns of white high above, Bella loosely clasped her fingers against her stomach and walked with slack, relaxed muscles. Her gaze wandered as she took in her surroundings with overhanging trees, low-growing shrubbery, and the reflection of them in the river. Smiling to herself, she breathed in the scents of wood, freshly cut grass, and greenery.

Bella pondered her time spent with Beatrice, who rejuvenated her and made her feel as though she could do anything she put her mind to.

Nature and spending time with loved ones brought out her inner child as if re-experiencing the love and nurture she'd never received as a child. Bella watched the play of a woman and a toddler. Their time together filled with laughs, hugs, and joy-filled love as the woman wrapped her arms tightly around the child. The woman stroked her child's hair, and the little girl squeezed the woman's cheeks when they pulled apart. It was amazing to watch the connection between mother and daughter; one Bella would never experience. Their love infusing the air around them, inviting Bella's lips to smile again and chuckle to herself. She took off her sandals and walked barefoot through the soft, green grass. The trees billowed around the park as the wind whistled an ominous tune, knowing that joy and laughter didn't last. In this moment, she immersed herself in nature, woodland, and soil to embrace and brave all the Earth's elements.

Peering at her watch, she crossed the road and made her way to work, humming a nonsensical tune to herself. She had a full day today, thanks to Liz who had brought in a few referrals. They included foster mothers with challenging foster children. Liz mentioned having limited time for counselling her own clients at work, and that these women wanted strategies and the space to vent. She secured new referrals via an Employee Assistance Program. Things were looking up.

As she drew closer to her building, she stopped in her tracks and gasped. Her surroundings felt surreal. With muscles tensed, her mind became fuzzy. Her hands clutched at her stomach as she shook her head while leaning against the wall.

On the side of the building, luckily hidden from passersby, was a huge sign printed in dark black onto the grey concrete surface for visitors to see. The sign read, "YOU'VE BEEN MARKED." *What the hell!* How was she going to see clients when this was in view?

Almost stumbling to the ground, warm hands pulled her up as she fought back rage. Her heart racing, she turned to find Mari offering her a reassuring smile. "Oh my God! Bella, who would do such a thing?"

Bella pulled herself upright and let go of Mari's hand. "I don't know, but I'm sick of being taunted. First by Jackson and now this."

The receptionist's eyes darkened. "I'll call the police."

"Thanks, Mari. You can speak to that detective, Marco. What am I going to do? I have my first client coming in an hour. She can't see the building like this."

Mari nodded and stroked Bella's hand. "Leave it with me. I'll explain this to your clients who I'm sure will understand the crazy vandals out there. Then I will buy a pot of paint and clear it up once I get the go-ahead from the police. Not to worry. I've got it all under control."

Bella grinned. "You are a Godsend. Thank you so much." Mari called the police and explained the incident.

They were about to head inside when Mari said, "Listen, why don't we go grab a coffee at that cafe across the road. The detective won't be here for at least half an hour, so we've got time to kill. I could do with one. Your first client's not due for a while. Let me shout you a coffee."

Bella nodded. "Thanks, Mari. Sounds good." Together they crossed the road. A chill rippled across her body. Would this ever end?

Marco arrived forty minutes later. Bella had rescheduled her first client for late afternoon due to the incident and to get the paint washed off. She opened the door and smiled in greeting when he knocked.

"Hello, Ms Carismo, or, aah, Bella." He looked more serious than usual as if something was wrong. "Some of my men are taking photos of the building. I've also arranged for the officers to check CCTV cameras in the area and question witnesses who might've seen something. Hopefully, it shouldn't take long to get that paint washed off."

"Thank you." She led him to the chair across from her own. He wore a tight black shirt under a fitted grey jacket with loose beige pants. He had stubble on his chin and dark circles under his eyes, as if he needed sleep. She couldn't help noticing the tautness and strong build of his shoulders and chest, with a fluttery sensation down her spine.

She tilted her head. "I'm sorry to take you away from your murder case."

"It's all good. I don't mind checking in from time to time." Their eyes lingered until Bella looked past him. "Tell me what's happened since I last saw you. Any other threats?"

"No, none."

"Do you think your client, Jackson, would do this?"

Bella sighed. "It's possible, but I can't be sure."

He nodded. "We'll question Jackson about his whereabouts for today." He exhaled. "We'll write up a report and, hopefully, your insurance will cover it. I assume you have building insurance?"

"Yes, I do. I'll get it sorted."

After further questioning, Marco said, "I thought you'd like to know that we've looked into Jackson's history, and given that this might be relevant to your safety, apparently a few women have reported him for assault. Did you know anything about that?"

Bella shook her head. "No, I didn't, but I do know that he hates me for ending our professional relationship."

His eyes darkened a moment, appearing miles away. He faced her, looking grim. "Are you sure you don't want to press charges against him?"

"I think he needs serious help rather than prison at this stage."

Marco cleared his throat. "Anyway, I've been assigned to your case."

Bella looked curiously at him. "Oh, but what about your murder case? Surely you don't have time for me too?" He fidgeted and turned away. "Detective? What are you not telling me?"

"I'm afraid that we'll have to consider a connection here."

Bella angled her head. "What do you mean?"

He hesitated. "Bridget's killer wrote 'You've Been Marked' on her body, in blood."

Bella froze. "What? Why didn't you tell me that before?"

"Until we question all those associated with the victim, we cannot provide too many details of a murder."

She chuckled. "You thought I was guilty, didn't you?"

He shook his head. "No, it's simply protocol. We cannot share any details until we've investigated further. Now that there seems to be a connection,

I'll have to assume that your stalker might be related to Bridget." He took a breath. "We'll keep searching, and hopefully, we'll work out what's going on." Rising from the seat, he shook Bella's hand, his eyes again fixated on hers. She ignored his gaze and turned away, leading him outside her office. Once the door shut behind her, she closed her eyes and put Marco out of her mind. It was comforting to know he'd be taking over her stalking case, but her inner terror at a possible connection to Bridget's murder made her want to flee for her life.

***

Later that night, Marco sat in his living room, drinking a beer while he rested his legs on the couch. He wished he could've kept his damn mouth shut. But he had to tell her about the connection and scare her. It was his job to investigate the connection. He hated to spook her, but he'd had no choice. He hated how her sadness became even more intense, giving her a deep sense of hopelessness. But he had a duty to tell her. She'd need to be on her guard. He could protect her and keep her safe, but he couldn't be there 24/7.

It was scary to think that her stalker had threatened her friend, Liz. He didn't want anyone to be the killer's next target, and doubted Bridget was a one-off kill. A murder of this calibre suggested that the killer possibly got pleasure out of the kill, which meant the police might need to look into past murders to see if they were connected.

He couldn't fathom how anyone would have a deep grudge against Bella. She looked like the type to give out her heart and soul to those around her. Her career in psychology said a lot about her too. *Damn!* Why couldn't he get her image out of his head? It was wrong to keep thinking about her, but he still wondered what she was doing now. Was she at home, sharing a meal with her boyfriend or was she reading a book? What were her likes and dislikes? He shook the thoughts out of his head and rose to have a cold shower.

Chapter Twenty-Eight

THE BULKY FIGURE

Four days later, on a Friday evening, Bella sat on Jamie's couch beside Martha, who was shaking as she drew a hand through her strawberry-blonde curls, her green eyes darkening.

Jamie had called her earlier that day to request Bella's help after Martha had received disturbing news. Bella agreed to help Martha, given she was still struggling with the separation from her husband.

Jamie had given them privacy and disappeared into her bedroom. The spacious home was ultra-modern with prominent art pieces hanging on the wall, open, bare windows with a view of the city skyline, plush rugs in the living room and bedrooms, a SMART TV and glass cabinets circling a surround-sound stereo system. All the finer things that money could buy, given that Jamie appreciated art and modern furniture.

Bella gave Martha a reassuring smile as she waited for her to share the latest development between her and her husband.

"That woman convinced George to move in with her, and now he has." She wiped away tears with a tissue, her body shivering. "He wants a divorce, but I'm not ready for that. I still have hope."

"I'm sorry, Martha. That must be hard to accept. Is George open to marriage counselling at all?"

She shook her head. "No, he's convinced he's in love with her." She rubbed her cheek. "He said he's not sure if he still loves me or not."

"He might be confused about his feelings right now. Maybe give it time. Negotiate with him about giving you time to process the separation, let alone a divorce."

"I said that, but he's still convinced he wants a divorce. I don't know what to do."

"Is there anyone else in your circle of family or friends who can speak to him? Perhaps explain how rushing things might not be the best thing."

Martha lifted her shoulder. "Maybe. He was always close to my brother. I could ask if he'd speak to him."

Bella swallowed. "That's good. It's worth a try." She shifted. "How long has George been living with his girlfriend?"

Martha squeezed her hands. "Only a few days."

Bella touched her arm. "Sometimes men cheat because they're afraid to ask for what they need in the relationship and might feel that something's missing. They seek it elsewhere, but over time, the fantasy of an affair might wear off. There is a chance that he might realise that reality and this other woman don't fit. There's also a chance of the opposite. For now, keep an open mind and focus on yourself. Take care of your health, Martha. You'll get through this."

Martha fixed her gaze on Bella. "I'll try, but I can't sleep and I can't eat. I've even taken a few days off work. If it wasn't for Jamie, I'd probably be more of a basket case and leave work altogether. Both of you have been great."

Bella's heart warmed. "If you still find you're not sleeping, perhaps see your doctor for sleep medication. Only temporary, though, so you're able to function at work. The more sleep you lose, the more depressed you'll feel. Think about it."

"I will. Thanks again for your support, Bella. Jamie's lucky to have you as a friend."

Jamie waltzed into the room. "I heard the utterings of my name."

Bella rose. "I think that's my cue to leave. It is getting late."

Martha got up and leaned forward, wrapping her arms around Bella. "Can we have another chat in the next few weeks? I'd like to tell you how I'm doing."

Bella beamed. "Of course. Any time. If you need to speak earlier than that, let Jamie know and I'll make myself available. You take care."

Martha nodded. "I'll be going to bed now. See you ladies."

As Martha left for her room, Jamie moved in closer. "How are things with you? I heard about the vandalism incident from Liz."

"I'm sorry. Liz called me later that day and I told her what happened. I knew she'd let you know. Besides, I can't be burdening you guys with these things."

Jamie pursed her lips. "I would like to know about every incident, no matter how small. Okay? No secrets between us. The police will eventually stop whoever is harassing you, and we will be right by your side." She angled her head. "I heard about that hot new detective of yours too."

Bella sighed. "He is not my hot detective. He is helping me with my case."

Jamie toyed with her fingers. "Doesn't he have a murder investigation too?"

Bella nodded. "I guess he might be handling both cases."

"Hmm, I wonder why."

"It's not what you think. He believes there might be a connection."

Jamie flinched. "Are you serious?"

Bella discussed the connection. "I don't want you to worry. He's got my back. Anyway, I have to go." She walked herself to the door as her friend followed. "I'll see you, Jamie."

"I'll walk with you to your car. It's dark outside. I have doubts about you being on your own, Bella. You should stay here tonight."

"I'll be fine."

As Jamie closed the door behind her, Bella waited. They walked to the end of Jamie's yard and Bella froze. Something wasn't right. The night grew silent and still as if holding its breath. The hair on her shoulders stood on end. Her whole body refused to move. Even her legs couldn't carry her as she stood frozen in her spot. The moon lit up the deserted street. Apart from a few cars, no-one was around. It must be the silence unnerving her. Then she saw him.

Jamie turned and made her way to Bella, then stopped. "What's wrong?"

Bella's whispered words were shaky. "Look over there. That man." A bulky-looking man wearing a leather jacket with a beanie and boots loomed in the distance, staring at Bella. His head tilted and then he pointed at her with a finger. He then directed it towards himself and moved it across his throat. He took a few steps towards her, zombie-like, grimacing then throwing his head back in a chuckle. Bella and Jamie backed away and headed slowly to her house.

"Let's get back inside. He's crazy," said Jamie.

Bella's throat tightened. Her hands were clammy. The man quickened his steps, carrying something in his hand. Bella's body shook, her mouth dry. He smirked. She shivered all over. The bulky man ran full force towards them. Jamie quickly opened the door and pushed Bella inside. She locked the door and peered through the blinds.

"He's standing in front of the house, but I don't know what he's doing. I am calling the police. We have to report this." Jamie grabbed her phone.

Bella's elbows pressed into her sides, making herself as small as possible. Her shoulders tightened and her breathing became shallower. She avoided looking through the curtains, her heart beating a mile a minute. She took calming breaths.

Jamie turned towards her. "He is gone now. Are you okay?"

Bella nodded slowly, her legs giving out on her. She tumbled to the floor. Jamie knelt beside her, holding her tightly.

Was that man her stalker or was he a crazy person with nothing better to do? It couldn't be a coincidence. She couldn't keep living this way, forever scared and not wanting to go outside. Something had to give.

Chapter Twenty-Nine

A THREAT

Bella sat on the sofa, her hands clasped across her stomach, cowering and quivering. Again, she took calming breaths. *"I am safe. I'm safe now. He can't hurt me. He can't hurt me,"* she said to herself. Images of her father flashed before her. She could never get those images of his bulky figure hovering over her, taunting her, injuring her over and over throughout her childhood.

Jamie sneaked up on her. Her body shuddering and her breath shallow again. "My God, Bella. You look so pale." She sat beside her and pulled her close, stroking her shoulder. "It's all fine. He is gone now, and the detective is on his way." Bella had no speech, her body frozen in shock. "I will make us a cup of tea." Jamie rose. Bella's surroundings appeared surreal. She had to be dreaming. It wasn't like last time when she was always walking on eggshells. She was safe and away from her family now.

Footsteps made her jump again. She looked up to face Martha who was rubbing her eyes. "What's happened, Bella?"

Bella briefly closed her eyes. *I am safe. I am safe.* When she opened them, Martha looked at her quizzically and sat on the armchair opposite. "This man outside. He was running towards us, and..." Bella stopped when Jamie carried over two mugs of tea and put them on the coffee table. Jamie explained the incident.

"Would you care for a tea, Martha? There is still plenty of water in the kettle."

"I'm fine, thanks. Are you guys okay? Bella here looks pretty shaken up."

Jamie sat next to Bella and asked, "Can I tell her about your situation?"

Bella nodded. "It's fine. Any friend of yours is a friend of mine."

Jamie disclosed Bella's stalking events as Martha placed a hand over her mouth, turning her head from side to side.

Bella wanted to be left alone. She needed the support, but why should those she loved be involved in this mess? She didn't know what she'd done to deserve this.

When the doorbell rang, Jamie answered the door. Marco stepped into the living room with his partner, Tim, and an officer.

Bella glanced into the kind eyes of Marco who sat on the couch beside her. His partner stood in the background with a stern expression on his face. The officer looked very young, his blue eyes looking her over.

"Can you tell me exactly what happened tonight?" Marco said.

Jamie recounted the incident and Bella added in bits and pieces, her voice slurring as if she was drunk. She had to get a hold of herself. She needed to be stronger than this. After everything she'd been through, this incident was nothing. Yet it shook her to the core, as if part of the past was returning.

"And can you give us a description of the man in question?" said Tim.

Bella swallowed. "He was a large man wearing a leather jacket with a beanie and boots. We couldn't see him clearly because he was a bit distant, but the threat he made was clear."

Marco turned to the officer. "I'd like you to canvas any nearby witnesses and locate CCTV in the area." He spoke on his phone and gave out instructions for the search. He ended the call and focused on Bella and Jamie. "My partner will canvas the area and search around your home. Stay indoors and we'll check it out. We won't be long."

After some time had passed, Marco and his partner knocked on the door and Jamie invited them back in.

Marco moved closer to Bella who stayed glued to the couch. His leg brushed hers. Her muscles relaxed. He put a comforting hand on her shoulder. She felt safe with him around, especially when he squeezed her shoulder like that. "So far, not a soul in sight. But I suggest you stay here for the night. I'll get the officer to keep surveillance outside to make sure the guy doesn't come back. We don't know the man's intentions, but he did threaten you. Given your current history of harassment, we have to assume this could be a connection and that the perpetrator wanted to send a message."

Bella turned towards him, lost in his dark eyes. Her skin flushed and her body felt weak from his closeness. She stammered with her next words. "I have no idea who's doing this to me, but I don't think he's going to stop anytime soon."

Marco touched his throat. "All I can suggest, Bella, is that you make sure you check your surroundings before going anywhere, and don't walk alone at night. Record every incident and let me know everything that happens, no matter how small." He got up and smiled reassuringly.

Bella rose too, her legs unsteady. "I'm sorry to bother you so late at night."

"Any time. It's my job."

Marco walked out with his partner and closed the door behind them while Bella hugged her body, a chill travelling down her legs.

Jamie led Bella to the bedroom. "Come on, you're sleeping in my room. I'll take the couch."

Martha shook her head. "No, listen. You take the other room. I'm happy to have the couch."

Bella intervened. "No, I'll be fine here."

Jamie gave her a stern look. "My goodness, Bella. You are obviously still rattled. I am happy to be here, both of you. Now off to bed. I will see you women in the morning. Goodnight."

Bella and Martha walked to their respective bedrooms and called it a night. Bella couldn't get the image of the man out of her head. He had looked threatening and dangerous, and no doubt if they hadn't run off, he would have most likely attacked them. She was sure he held a weapon. She replayed the scene over and over until it rolled into her father hurting her. She wrestled with the flashback, grounding herself and pushing it down. She used meditative breathing to help her finally fall asleep in the early hours of the morning.

Chapter Thirty

A FUN OUTLET

*B*ella *ran as fast as she could on her short legs, looking behind her every few seconds. The footsteps were getting closer and closer, her heart racing. If she could get out of the living room and outside into the street, she'd be safe. She was a fast runner, but he was faster. He came in behind her, the gap closing between them. A strong hand grabbed her and yanked her by the shoulder. A stabbing pain settled as he threw her down on the ground. "You bitch." He sat on top of her, weighing her down, and slapped her twice. Her face stung and the slap bloomed red.*

"I'm sorry Daddy for breaking the vase."

His face was menacing. His teeth gritted, wrinkles lining his cheek. As his eyes distended, his bulk squashed her small body. "That vase was valuable, from my dear grandmother, and now it's gone. Gone forever, and you have to pay. You have to pay.”

He held his hands around her throat until she passed out.

Bella woke up in a sweat, gasping. Her body was hot and quaking. She lifted herself slowly out of bed and breathed in and out. In and out. *It was just a stupid dream.* She was safe in her own home. Her father could no longer hurt her. She was safe.

Shaking off the dream as she had many times before, she pushed down her nerves and headed to the kitchen. She made herself breakfast—jam toast and coffee—then after a warm shower, she retreated to her room and meditated for thirty minutes. She always felt grounded after her meditation, and the practice had allowed her to stay sane throughout the day. She wouldn't let the past affect her present. It was still there, but she'd always managed with the support of her friends and work. What more did she need?

Love. Her mind insisted. Love from a real family. She'd never had any of that, except from her aunt and her friends. She still craved for her parents' love. The empty pit inside her threatened to rise up, but she distracted herself. She was great at distraction. The meditation helped her make some semblance of a life on her own in spite of the trauma. The acceptance of her past was a work in progress.

It was a Sunday morning, two days after the incident with Jamie, and Bella had no plans other than grocery shopping. Yesterday, she stayed at Jamie's place for the day and spent time with Liz and Martha as well, but last night, Bella had insisted she return home. Her life couldn't be put on hold simply because a madman was after her. No, she was better than that. Today, she didn't want to do anything and preferred to be on her own. When her phone rang, she almost didn't answer it.

"Hi Liz. How are you?"

"Great, girl. I thought we could do something fun today. Just you and me. Jamie's on call with Martha at work."

Bella's shoulders deflated. "Thanks for the offer, but I'm not in the mood to do anything. Besides, I saw you yesterday."

"Hmm, so I'm boring to you, am I?" Liz jested.

Bella chuckled lightly. "Never boring, Liz. But I just need time to recover after Friday night."

"I understand, but you need fun in your life, girl. You can't be serious all the time. As a psychologist, you know that's not healthy. I'm coming over to take you out."

Bella knew when Liz made up her mind, nobody could change it. She would never relent and would harp on it all day. In the end, Bella didn't have the energy to argue with her. "Fine. Come over then."

"Great. I'll see you soon."

She hung up and pressed her hands against her head, fighting off a migraine. She wanted to be alone.

Bella and Liz walked out of the cinema Nova in Carlton that afternoon. The sun warmed her skin as she relived the sad love story between the movie's characters, a part of her wanting that kind of love. Maybe she wasn't built that way. She was in her twenties and had yet to have a long-term relationship. As soon as a man started to get serious, she would quickly end it. She didn't deny the fear of commitment, but did she want to be alone for the rest of her life?

She breathed in the warm air and watched strollers passing by the cafes, restaurants, and clothing stores along Lygon Street. Liz steered them into the University Cafe.

Bella sat opposite Liz who was already calling a waiter towards her. He scurried over and took their orders of wine, a Margherita pizza for Liz, and a Capricciosa pizza for Bella. The smells of oregano, basil, and tangy tomatoes filled the air, making her mouth water. Freshly brewed coffee enticed her senses too.

Liz clasped her hands together after the waiter left. "I loved the characters in the movie. They were so authentic, but the movie was a bit slow in the beginning. Don't you just love that romantic tension between a couple?"

Bella shrugged. Her mind veered towards Marco. She wrestled it down into submission and insisted it behave. She focused on Liz. "I suppose."

"Anyway, a colleague of mine is having a masquerade party for her birthday. You have to come."

Bella averted her eyes. "I don't know, Liz. It's hard to get into the mood these days."

"You promised me you'd come the next time, and next time is in two weeks. Please, please, please come. I know you'll have fun. You can bring that hot detective if you like."

Bella shook her head, a sense of guilt overwhelming her. As a friend, she owed it to Liz to at least show up to parties once in a while. She wasn't being very supportive of Liz lately. Liz was a social butterfly, the complete opposite of Bella. "You know it is a conflict of interest to be socialising with the detective." She took a breath. "Fine, I'll come."

Liz grinned and her eyes lit up. "Oh, you are a Godsend. I'm sure it'll take your mind off things, but you're still spooked, aren't you?"

Bella nodded. "I appreciate what you're doing by trying to take my mind off things, and I'm sure the detective will get a lead."

Liz slid her chair closer to the table and wrinkled her nose. "But?"

"But what?"

"I know there's more you wanted to say, but never mind. Did you even sleep last night? You look pretty tired, girl."

"Not much, but it's fine. I'm sure I'll sleep tonight without—" Bella stopped short.

Liz gazed at her with focus. "Are you having nightmares again?" Bella stayed silent. "Tell me about it. It'll help to get it off your chest."

"I'd rather not get into it, Liz."

"Listen, I know you mentioned how your parents were abusive, so was it about them?" Silence. "Bella, you need to open up about your dreams, your experiences. This is the only way you'll be able to get a handle on your memories."

"I know, you're right, but I have to move past it, Liz. I can't let my father control my life anymore. He did so many things to me, and I really can't get into the specifics."

"I understand that, but at least let someone carry that burden with you. My God, Bella. You're an amazing psychologist, but what about caring for yourself as much as you care for your clients?"

"That's sometimes the case with us therapists. We're better at helping others than ourselves, but I promise I will get help once this madness is over."

She sighed. "Good. I will remind you of that once all this stuff is over."

Bella smiled when the waiter brought over the wine. The pizza arrived a few minutes later. Bella watched Liz with admiration, knowing that without her, she'd be completely lost in the world. Her support network kept her strong.

Liz scratched her chin. "About the party." She cleared her throat. "The only thing is, Claudia will most likely be there. She's my colleague's friend."

Oh, wonderful! Bella suppressed a groan with a bite of pizza.

Chapter Thirty-One

AMAZING NEWS

The following Saturday, Bella sat inside the Williamstown Hospital cafeteria with Martha. Jamie was busy with patients, and Martha contacted Bella. She had news.

Martha stood rigid, her eyes lighting up as she peered into the distance.

"So don't keep me hanging, Martha. What's the good news?"

She rubbed her hands together. "Jamie knows about it, but I wanted to let you know, given how supportive you've been these past few weeks. I couldn't have got through my separation without you."

"And?" Bella asked. She wondered why Martha hesitated in sharing her news when she was obviously ecstatic about it. What held her back? Mixed feelings?

"George and I are working things out. He's moved back home, but it'll be a while before I forgive him, if ever. We're looking into marital counselling."

Bella's heart lifted. "That's amazing news, Martha. What happened exactly?"

She held her head down briefly. "Well, you know how George moved in with that wretched woman a couple of weeks ago?"

"Sure, you mentioned that."

"He realised that living with her wasn't the way he thought it would be. He said she was possessive and clingy, crying every time he caught up with his friends at the pub once a week. He couldn't live that way, and realised he still loved me. He moved out of there, but she threatened to kill herself."

Bella knew the type. "Emotional blackmail?"

"Yep, but he didn't fall for it. Once he told her he still loved me and wanted to make a go of it with me, she got angry and vindictive. He knew she was manipulating him, so he got out of there quickly."

Bella had an uneasy feeling about women like that. Crazed women who only knew how to trick people through manipulation and passive-aggressive behaviour. Innocent people always got hurt. "So once he got packing and physically left her, how did the woman appear then?"

"He said she'd calmed down and seemed to accept the situation."

"It's amazing that he realised she wasn't the woman for him. Now, it's a matter of working out where things went wrong." Her eyebrows knit together. "Did you ever see the woman?"

Martha shook her head. "No, thank God. She's obviously a very insecure nutter." She smiled. "I'd really like us to be friends and keep in touch. Is that okay? You're exactly what I need in my life, Bella. A stable rock who's supported me throughout all this."

Bella's chest lifted. "Thanks. I'd like us to be friends too. We have to have dinner one night."

"I'd like that," Martha said.

When lunch was over, they embraced. Bella walked to the exit and headed to her car. She smiled at the thought of Martha possibly working things out. She deserved to be happy, and marriage was a huge commitment to destroy over a woman who was clearly a manipulator. She obviously had issues if she was threatening to kill herself. George realised he already had a woman who was real, authentic, honest, and who loved him.

As she used her fob to unlock her car, she felt she was being watched. She scanned her surroundings and didn't notice anything out of the ordinary. Lately, she was always looking over her shoulder, but she got respite from Martha's good news after living in fear all these weeks. She had made a new friend in Martha. Hopefully their marriage would work out in the end.

The person watched, with hands clenched as Bella walked out from lunch with Martha, her new besty. The person's pulse elevated and ears pounded as Bella drove off. "Bitch!! The next part of my plan will shock that stupid cow to the core."

Chapter Thirty-Two

AN UNEXPECTED VISITOR

Bella smiled to herself when rising from her meditation corner at home, flashing back to the healthy glow on Martha's face. It was contagious, and she couldn't help yearning for that same joy. Bella hoped that Martha's husband wouldn't cheat on her again and that he had learned his lesson. Yet those who cheated sometimes repeated their mistake due to either having a predisposition to it or finding it easier to do the second time around. Martha didn't deserve to be treated that way, and he'd better not hurt her again.

Stepping into the kitchen, Bella turned on the electric kettle and pulled out a mug. As she grabbed the sugar bowl, the doorbell rang.

Putting aside the bowl, Bella swung open the door and angled her head at the unexpected visitor. "Detective? This is a surprise. Come on in."

Marco smiled. "Sorry to bother you, but I was checking in, making sure you're okay after the incident at your friend's house."

He walked inside and Bella ushered over to her couch. She sat beside him with space between them. His eyes roamed the living area, staring at the patio outside with the glass double doors giving a view of the backyard. Bella savoured this time of year when she could open up the doors and let a breeze come into the house during the spring season. It gave the house an open-plan and spacious ambience.

"You have a beautiful house. I especially like the patio outside. Great for the spring season, and today's an absolutely gorgeous day." His eyes fixed on her for a moment, but Bella turned away, her face blushing. The tingles in her fingers and chest almost overwhelmed her as she waited for Marco to say more. "How have you been?"

Bella turned back towards him as he shifted closer towards her on the couch. Her breath shallowed. "I've been busy with a few new clients at the practice. After that social media post about my credibility, I'd lost a few of them. Luckily, I haven't had any new posts slander my name."

He nodded. "That's good to hear." He gazed past her. "I thought I'd let you know that we're following up on leads with Bridget's murder."

"Anything you can share?"

Marco shook his head. "Sorry. Unless it's relevant to a court case or an arrest, I can't say anything else at this stage. The person we're looking at is obviously smart and well-organised, staging the scene like a personal vendetta. With uncontrolled rage. Would you know of anyone who would target Bridget?"

"No, no-one I know." Bella rose. "I was making myself a cup of tea. Would you like one?"

Marco turned away for a moment. "Sure. I mean, I might have a few more questions."

Bella headed to the kitchen and took out a second mug. Her hands shook as she took out the milk from the fridge, sensing Marco's strong presence in the living room. She glanced over at him. He was perusing her bookshelf. The moment of inattention made her almost drop her teaspoon, but she managed to grab it mid-air. Once finished, she carried the two mugs of tea on a tray with a small plate of Kingston biscuits and set it on the coffee table.

Marco turned towards her. "You have loads of interesting books here. The treatment of clients with personality disorders. The co-dependency of relationships. The anxious mind, and a lot about holistic health too. You're obviously spiritual, aren't you?"

Bella sat back on the couch and sipped her tea. "I like to do spiritual things, meditate, energy work, read up on Buddhist philosophy. It's got me through a lot of things."

Marco's gaze held. He sat down and gripped his mug. "I take it you've been through a lot."

Bella crossed and uncrossed her legs. "What makes you say that, detective?"

Marco chuckled. "I can sense some reservation, a keen sense to please others and mediate rather than draw out conflict. You find strength in helping others. But you often ignore your own needs because you feel like a burden. Am I right so far?"

Bella blushed and smoothed down her jeans. She hid her hands in her pockets and bit her lip. How dare he presume things about her, even if he was right? She barely knew the guy and he had the nerve to open her up like a book. This was too much, but she fought back her nerves. "So, you're profiling me now, detective?"

He crinkled his nose. "I'm sorry. I didn't mean to make you uncomfortable. I was out of line."

Bella rose. "Excuse me a moment." Heading to the bathroom and turning on the tap, she stared in the mirror at her light green eyes and dimples. She rubbed at her cheeks to add colour to her paleness. Her body was shaking as her father's voice resounded heavily in the forefront of her mind. Her mother stood back with a bottle of whisky in her hands. Time seemed to stand still.

"You are only here to please us and nothing more. You don't serve much of a purpose but to do only what we tell you. Others have more value and worth than you, you piece of shit."

Marco's voice brought her back to the present. "Bella, are you okay in there?"

She washed her face quickly, not giving thought to water overflowing out of the basin and onto the floor. "Coming," she said. As she turned towards the door, her foot slipped in the water and she fell on her back with a strong thud, knocking her head on the floor. She scraped her arm against the edge of the door. Dizzy with pain, a blurred vision of Marco stared down at her.

Chapter Thirty-Three

A STRONG CONNECTION

Marco rushed into the bathroom and pulled Bella up. He put his arm around her and walked her to the living room, setting her down on the couch. "My God, Bella! Are you okay? What happened?"

Bella was nauseous. Her arm stabbed with pain, and she gritted her teeth. Her head felt heavy as she took calming breaths. *I'm okay. I'm safe now!* "Sorry. I just slipped and grazed my arm."

Marco kneeled opposite her. He leaned over and grabbed her arm, shaking his head. "Wait here. I'll get some disinfectant or see what else you have in your bathroom."

"Thanks." Bella bowed her head, sinking into the softness of the couch underneath her legs. The dizziness ceased. How stupid she was to have slipped in the bathroom. As if the humiliation of Marco's profiling wasn't enough. Now, he had to watch her act like a fool. All because of that stupid voice inside her head that occasionally reared itself when she was triggered. A lot of things triggered her, but as a psychologist, she could handle all that. *I didn't handle that well...* Maybe she would actually see a therapist like she had told Liz.

Marco returned with a few pieces of cotton wool and Dettol to disinfect the wound. He dabbed the liquid on to the cotton wool and pressed it gently to her wound. He watched her with a serious gaze. He parted his lips then closed them, swallowing. Her heart hammered, and she was aware of Marco's strong musky scent while he tended to her. She ignored the electrical jolt in her back, but her knees lost strength.

He looked up at her "There. All done." He dropped the dirty cotton wool into the rubbish bin in the kitchen then set the disinfectant on the table.

"I'll be fine now. I'm sure you have better things to do today. I don't need babysitting."

Marco lowered his head, his shoulders slumping. "Again, I'd just like to say how sorry I am about before. My friends tell me I should learn to be less analytical, an unfortunate trait of mine. I didn't mean any offense. Sometimes this job gets to you." He rose but hesitated in moving towards the door.

Bella put it behind her and shrugged. "It's fine. You obviously have a knack for profiling and figuring people out. I can probably figure you out too."

He beamed. "I'd like to see you try."

Bella got up from the couch, standing across from him only a small distance between them. "Is that a challenge, Mr Detective?"

He moved closer. "I guess it is."

For a moment, Bella's tongue didn't want to move but she cleared her mind and rose to the challenge. "Hmm. Let's see now. "You're sensitive and expressive, as you've shown. But as a youngster, you were neglected in some way and that created this sensitivity and need for love. You yearn for acceptance from others but still feel this emptiness inside because what you want, others so far haven't been able to give it to you. You're very creative and crave emotional depth and deep discussion." She might've clinched it as his face reddened, and his eyes lingered on hers.

"Wow. That's amazing. Except for the emptiness part."

Bella wondered if he had the love of a strong woman and no longer felt empty if he'd found the love he possibly craved. It was none of her business, but the way he was looking at her suggested he was very much single. She could barely breathe.

Bella clasped her hands together, ignoring the magnetic pull to Marco. It took all her strength not to move in and kiss him on those thick, rosy lips. It took all her strength not to touch his muscular shoulders and chest, and have his arms wrapped tightly around her. He was a detective, and she couldn't get involved when he was working on her case. *Control yourself, Bella. He's not only a detective but way out of your league. He'd never be interested in you that way, anyway.* "Well, I guess I was mostly right."

He relaxed his posture. His eyes glossed over her with a softened gaze. He took half a step forward and gently touched her shoulder. His hand lingered.

Bella became aware of her own heartbeat. She felt warm with goose bumps prickling across her body. She ached to touch him, so rested her own hand on his. She couldn't help but stare deeply into his eyes in the same way he was scrutinising her. She shifted and he leaned in, stroking her cheek as Bella closed her eyes to savour the tingling, gentle sensation of his hand on her cheek. She wanted Marco, and it was so very wrong.

When Marco wrapped an arm around her waist to draw her in closer, Bella's mind turned to her previous relationship with a man who first appeared to be a gentleman but ended up cheating.

He had also been a compulsive liar. She barely knew Marco and letting down her guard now would risk her getting hurt or even worse, abandoned. She'd had enough of that to last her a lifetime.

She quickly came to her senses and pulled away. Bella rushed to the door. "I think you'd better leave, Detective Marco. I have a busy day today."

He bowed his head. "I'm sorry. I crossed the line. It won't happen again."

With a few steps, he was out the door. Bella quickly closed it. As she watched him drive away, her skin prickled with danger. She suddenly felt very cold and alone. She looked out the patio windows. Was that someone moving in the bushes? Surely, it had to be her imagination. There was nobody around. She pulled the blinds closed, locking the door and sat on the couch, cowering.

Chapter Thirty-Four

A TRACE

Marco sat in the passenger seat while Tim drove faster than the speed limit. They'd received an anonymous tip about the man who'd scared Bella in front of Jamie's house and got his location. His hands fidgeted as they neared their destination, eager to exit the car.

Tim parked in front of a weathered, brick house with an untended lawn and wilting flowers. An overhanging tree blocked the side window.

Marco and Tim walked along a cracked, concrete path and banged on the door, waiting. Marco's hands clenched with the long wait. Was anyone even home? He knocked on the door again.

A strongly-built man with dishevelled hair and red eyes opened the door. He was tucking his shirt inside his jeans, obviously drug-affected. At the sight of them, he flinched.

"Mr Arthur Jamies?" Marco said.

He swallowed and looked behind him. "Who wants to know?"

He flashed his badge. "I'm Detective Senior Constable, Marco Petrazini and this is Detective Senior Constable, Tim Wittens. We have a few questions for you."

"Got nothing to say."

"We received an anonymous tip that you harassed a young woman and got paid well for it."

His head turned at the sound of movement behind him. He froze.

"Hey, honey. I miss your sexy body. Finish up will ya," said a girl who appeared to be under the age of consent.

Marco shouted, "How old are you, Miss?"

"Fifteen. Why?" The girl obviously had no clue about age of consent.

Marco grabbed the man whose eyes widened like saucers. "Mr Jamies, you're under arrest pertaining to the Crimes Act for having sex with a minor. You're coming to the station with us."

The man said nothing, his shoulders deflating. He turned to the girl. "Get me a damn lawyer."

❧❧❧❧❧❧❧ ❦❦❦❦❦❦

Later that day, Mr Arthur Jamies admitted to being hired by a woman named Claudia. Marco secured a warrant to search his email and phone records.

He stood in a room with a forensics expert, John, whose lanky frame barely fit his ergonomic chair in the cramped office.

John clicked away, digging into the background of Arthur, who had been communicating with Claudia, but the messages were rather cryptic. He had no criminal history, and on his phone, he'd sent messages to Claudia discussing the job he had on the night he scared Bella. He admitted to vandalising Bella's building too. Some people would do anything for money.

John turned to Marco. "You wanted me to check CCTV near Bella's building when it was vandalised?"

"Yes, please."

He searched into the different networks and leaned forward, keying in code to his heart's content. "Nothing, so far."

"Keep digging within a ten-mile radius." They needed confirmation that it was Mr Jamies vandalising the building, and to make sure he wasn't protecting anyone else.John shook his head. "These perps have plenty of time on their hands, nothing better to do. But don't worry, I'll find your man, to confirm it's your guy."

At that moment, Tim walked into the office. Marco explained their discovery. "Let's question Bella first and see if she knows this woman, Claudia.

See if there's a possible motive. Then we'll bring Claudia in."

"Shouldn't we be speaking to Claudia first?"

Marco needed to make sure Bella was okay. He had a job to do after all. "Let me ring Bella." Was he losing objectivity here?

The person huffed. "Damn cops. That bastard Jamies better not say anything. "No-one cares, anyway. I've got new plans. No price is too high."

Chapter Thirty-Five

A MASQUERADE PARTY

The Saturday of the masquerade party arrived all too quickly for Bella's liking. She pulled out her fitted satin dress, stiletto shoes, and intricate Venetian mask which featured black and gold patterns surrounding the spaces for the eyes. She had been able to purchase the accessories online at the last minute.

Bella wondered if she'd know anyone else at the party. Liz would most likely be busy socialising with other social workers who'd been invited. Bella couldn't expect Liz to keep her company the whole time.

She looked at herself in the mirror. The black stretch jersey dress was adorned with corded lace on the bodice and featured a heart-shaped neckline. It was off the shoulder and tight-fitted around the waist to display her slim curves. The length of the dress touched the floor, but her stiletto shoes lifted it slightly. She almost felt beautiful in this dress, and an image of Marco penetrated her thoughts. A part of her wished she was dressing especially for him. What would he think of her in this dress? Pushing out her thoughts, she moved away from the mirror and finished getting ready.

It was a lavish affair for a birthday party, and Bella had mixed feelings about attending this celebration, but she had promised Liz she'd go. She let Liz know not to expect too much of her with future parties. She could manage one night. She often told her clients to dare to seek out a task outside of their comfort zone, and she could do that too. She'd been through much worse over the years.

Liz arrived at her house an hour later. She walked to the door and answered it, greeting Liz. "You're just on time. Let me grab my bag."

She whistled. "You look gorgeous girl. Loving that dress."

"Thanks, Liz. You look gorgeous too. What an amazing dress you're wearing." It was a bright red dress that fell to her ankles with a plunging neckline and thin straps. A long split on the side of the dress put her tanned and toned legs on display. Never too flashy for Liz.

Liz lifted her dress as she walked inside. "Anyway. No rush. We get there when we get there."

Bella grabbed her black clutch and joined Liz outside. She managed to sit in Liz's car, a sporty red Mitsubishi Lancer, without rumpling her dress too much. Liz drove over the speed limit as usual, but she felt somewhat safe with her friend. It was only a short drive to Newport, but butterflies in her stomach made her jittery. The social aspect of parties always unnerved her.

Liz pulled up outside her colleague's house and stepped out of the car. They made their way along the concrete path to the brick-rendered house, between an immaculate front garden filled with coloured brush, hedging, a bird fountain, and low-hanging trees. Classical music sounded in the distance as Liz rang the doorbell. A woman with a flowing blue chiffon dress and a gold eye mask answered the door.

"Is that you, Penny, underneath that mask?" Liz asked.

The woman took off the mask. "Oh, yes, darling, it's me. You both look smashing in those outfits. Come on in."

They stepped inside and walked down the narrow foyer. They entered a large living room filled with dangling twinkling lights around the walls and down from the ceiling in a black and gold colour theme. Drapes of silk covered some of the furniture, and glass vases were filled with feathers and beads. Masks hung on walls and glitter and sequins had been sprinkled on the tables adorned with satin tablecloths.

Food of every variety lay on the tables: potato chips, pretzels, vol au vents, crab puffs, avocado wrapped in prosciutto, gourmet cheeses and crackers, caviar, and stuffed mushrooms. Another table was filled with a variety of other foods, savoury snacks, and assorted wines and liquors.

Guests came in sporadically as Liz and Bella tried some of the gourmet foods, filling them up on a plate. Bella poured herself a glass of wine. She was mesmerised by the intricate Venetian costumes. Some guests wore old-fashioned hoop dresses while others wore more modern attire. The men wore black suits and ties.

Bella's phone buzzed inside her bag. She retrieved it and answered. "Detective. This is a surprise."

"I've had a few leads with your stalking case, particularly the man who tried to scare you and vandalised your building too."

Bella looked at Liz who turned to her with a frown. "What leads?"

"We found the man responsible for the vandalism and the scare in Jamie's street. We need to question you about a woman named Claudia. I understand you have a history with her?"

Bella cringed. Although, she wasn't too surprised. She had wondered all along if Claudia was involved.

"Yes, I do. I worked with her in her practice a few years ago."

"We'd like to ask you a few questions about Claudia. At this stage, that's all I can tell you. We need to see you now due to timelines, and to rule certain things out."

"I'm not home. I'm at a masquerade party. Claudia's apparently coming here too. She's friends with the host. Can't this wait until tomorrow?"

"Not really. I can meet you wherever you are but please be discreet and don't say anything to anyone, including Claudia. It'll give us a chance to watch her too. This is routine questioning. Is there an address?"

Bella recited the location of the party. She hung up. Liz was looking at her strangely.

"The hot detective, ha? He's coming here now?"

Bella nodded. "Can you let the host know that a friend of mine is coming?"

"What's going on?"

Bella shrugged. "Can't say at this stage, Liz. Please don't ask anything else."

Liz nodded then disappeared into the crowd.

Bella waited near the snack table, watching strangers walk in and mingle. A sickening sensation churned her stomach as she turned and sipped on her wine. She probably should eat a bit more food before drinking to her heart's content. Liz had been out of sight for a while. *When was Liz getting back?*

She hated being at this party on her own. Luckily, nobody noticed yet.

Liz finally returned. "All good." They engaged in deep discussion and further nibbled at the snacks while Liz introduced her to a few people from work. Marco entered the room. He was here with his partner, Tim dressed in suitable costume attire but without the masks. They must've had emergency masquerade costumes back at the station. Bella couldn't help but smile at the thought. She waved them over after taking off her mask.

"Hello, ladies." His eyes trailed Bella from head to toe, his expression blazing. "I take it I am speaking to Liz there too."

"Detective," said Liz as she took off her mask then started up a conversation with his partner.

"Hello, Detective," said Bella ignoring the fluttery feeling in her stomach and dry mouth. She clasped her hands tight together.

"You look beautiful tonight, Bella," Marco said softly.

"Thanks. You look good, too. How did you find a costume so soon?" She felt herself blushing, entranced at the well-cut suit and tie and the hint of stubble on his chin. He stared deeply into her eyes and drew closer towards her. She was drawn to him. *This isn't right. You're being silly. Had too much wine.*

He chuckled. "You'd be surprised what the police station has in holding." His eyes roamed briefly. "Is Claudia here yet?"

Bella shook her head. "I don't think so." She looked around and noticed two men watching her. She was being paranoid. *Marco said he caught the guy, right?*

"Tell me everything you know about Claudia," Marco insisted. Bella explained their history to him. "And when was the last time you saw her?"

"The last time was when she wanted me to join her practice a few weeks ago. She might've also stolen my necklace." Bella explained the details.

Marco asked a few more questions about Claudia. Bella could barely concentrate as he gazed at her with his smiling eyes. The song *True* by Spandau Ballet began playing over the speakers, one of her favourites.

Marco glazed over her and held out his hand. "Why don't we blend in? Would you care to dance, Ms Carismo?"

Bella hesitated, wondering if it was a good idea. She turned to Liz who was deep in conversation with the other detective.

"Okay."

She took his hand, and he led her to the centre of the living room where a few people danced to the ballad.

Marco's arms wrapped around her, and she placed her hands on his shoulders. She avoided his eyes, feeling them on her but if she looked at him, she might lose her resolve to keep things professional. Her whole body was on fire from the tightness of his embrace and the way he stroked the small of her back. His strong cologne drew her in further. Bella got swept away by the music. She accidentally glanced at his mouth. His lips were apart as if he wanted to say something. The softness of his breathing and the gentle touch of his hands made her weak at the knees.

When the music stopped, they pulled apart and moved towards the food table. She took a sip of her wine, feeling a little flushed, and realised that the two men who had been staring had disappeared.

Claudia arrived fashionably late, holding on to her mask. She obviously needed to make her grand entrance.

Chapter Thirty-Six

A PARTY TRICK

Bella saw Liz circling the room, engaging with colleagues. She made her way back to her, laughing.

"What's going on?" Bella drew a hand through her hair. "

"Penny's got a few people hitting a piñata in the other room. She's been telling the hitters to imagine swiping their enemy." Bella tilted her head and scrunched her nose. She didn't really get party games and "swiping their enemy" seemed a bit extreme. "Where's the hot detective?"

Bella sighed. "Can you stop saying that, Liz? It's getting old." She looked around. "He and his partner were watching Claudia for a bit then left to follow up on a few things. He was being cryptic."

"Claudia? What's really going on?"

Oh, damn! She wasn't supposed to mention her name. "I'm not allowed to say, Liz."

Liz placed a manicured hand over her hip. "Come on, girl. It's me here. I won't go blabbing to anyone else. I'll be discreet. I might be able to help."

Liz was right. She needed her support right now. "Claudia's a person of interest." She whispered the details as Liz's eyes widened.

"Do you really think that Claudia's your stalker?"

Bella shrugged. "I don't know, but we'll eventually find out." Her mobile phone buzzed with a text notification. Retrieving it from her bag, she checked the screen and cringed. The message said, *I'm watching you everywhere!*

Liz leaned towards her, staring at the screen. "My goodness, Bella. You have to let the detective know about this. Call him." Her eyes scanned the room. "There's Claudia. She's got her bag over her shoulder. Maybe you can distract her while I grab the phone inside her bag. I can quickly check to see if she sent you that text."

"You expect me to make nice chit chat with her? We hate each other."

"Talk about the practice or something. I don't know. You'll figure it out." Liz started moving forward. Bella tried to follow but was stalled by a man who bumped into her and spilled wine over the front of her dress. She drew back.

The man muttered, "So sorry," and left to make his way to another room. *Jerk!*

"What a creep," said Liz. She had witnessed the spill and returned. "He could've offered to pay for dry cleaning."

"It's okay. Where's the bathroom?"

"I'm not sure. This house is huge. There's probably more than one." Her eyes roamed the room. "Oh, damn, I've lost Claudia. Wait here. I'll try to find her and ask Penny about the bathroom. Don't go anywhere yet. I'll be back."

Liz headed to the piñata room, so Bella waited, feeling dirty with the huge stain on her dress. Time passed by but Liz still hadn't shown up. Rather than waiting in frustration, Bella headed to the piñata room herself and spotted Penny. A burly man was swiping at the piñata, but the goodies still didn't want to come out of it.

"Hi love. Having fun?" Penny asked.

"I am, thanks. Have you seen Liz?"

Penny looked around. "Not sure. She was here a moment ago, but I don't know where she's gone." *Probably met a hot guy herself*, she thought. Staring at her dress, Penny added, "Oh, your dress is wet. I've got a dryer in the bathroom. Use that."

"Can you tell me where the bathroom is."

Penny pointed. "Just out of this room and to your left. It's at the end of that corridor."

"Thanks," said Bella. She smiled and made her way towards the toilet, hoping to get this wine stain out of her dress. Luckily, it was black and not very noticeable, but she reeked of wine and could feel the dampness through the fabric.

The hallway was narrow, and the space was dark and silent. Tinsel and decorations hung down from blue tack marked on the walls. All the doors to rooms she passed were closed. She found one open to her left, but it wasn't the bathroom. She turned at the sound of a squeaky floorboard but saw no-one behind her. A coldness in the air made her skin prickle. She stared at her feet, making quick strides to alleviate her uneasiness. Bella was close to the end of the corridor when a whiff of aftershave caught her by surprise. That was strange. Nobody was around. Maybe someone was in the bathroom. As she reached that space and stepped inside, she felt a sharp stab in her neck.

She fell into someone's arms and gasped. Feeling woozy, strong arms held her as she was led into a bedroom. She tried to regain her mobility but her head was fuzzy and her limbs weren't responding. The room spun around her, and her vision blurred. She was pushed onto a bed, her head rolling to the side. Looking up, a silver mask on what appeared to be a male face hovered over her. He was watching her, hesitating. He looked at his phone. Wasn't that the same man who had stared at her earlier? The one who had spilled wine on her? The eyes looked the same through the eye holes. Was this her stalker?

"Who are...you? What....d..o...you want?"

"This is just a taste of what's to come. It will only get worse from here."

She didn't know what he was talking about. He approached closer to her on the bed, sat on her and took off her mask. She held her stomach and moved her head to the side again. Her body trembled with fear. There was a sour taste in her mouth, and she wanted to escape more than anything, but whatever he had injected her with had sapped all of her strength. Her body was paralysed but she had to stay awake.

The man swung out his arm and punched her hard in the face, bruising her eye and cheek. He moved his hands up to her breasts and squeezed them. She couldn't shift her body or fight him because of the drug.

"No, don't. P..lease. No."

He smirked and ignored her when he lifted up her dress, kneading her thighs and trailing his hands down to her knees. He pulled her underwear down and spread her legs out. She felt useless, unable to stop him. She had no feeling in her body, and this man was about to rape her. *No*. She couldn't take this again. *No, no.*

A noise in the distance got her attention. A blurry figure pulled the man off of her. Was that Liz? She quickly pulled Bella's underwear back up and her dress down. The man seemed to have recovered and rose from the ground. "Liz. The... m..an," Bella said.

Liz turned and the man struck her hard across the cheek. She winced for a brief moment before retrieving the nearby lamp and pulling it out of its socket. She struck him across his face with the lamp. His body went limp as he fell on the floor.

Liz neared her on the bed and got her sitting up. "My god, Bella. Are you okay, girl?"

"Can't...move my body."

"I'll call an ambulance. Hang tight. You'll be fine." She called from the bedside phone, instructing the ambulance where to go, then made another call. Bella couldn't make out what Liz was saying.

The room spun around Bella. Liz returned to her and stroked her face looking extremely concerned. Penny came into the room. "I was worried about both of you taking so long in the bathroom. I came to find you when I heard the noise." Liz explained the situation to her colleague. Everything suddenly went black.

Chapter Thirty-Seven

A LOST LEAD

Bella's body ached and felt weak the next day. She lay on her couch, hugging a blanket while Liz and Jamie cooked lunch in the kitchen. She shivered in spite of the blanket.

Images of last night came to the forefront of her mind. She'd had a weird feeling at the party when those two men had been watching her. She thought nothing of it until it was too late. Too late to tell the detective of her uneasiness.

Her mind shut down and she dozed off, only to be awoken by a loud voice. It was Claudia at the door having a screaming match with Liz.

"Bella doesn't want you here, so get lost," said Liz.

"This isn't your place. Let me speak to her."

"She is sleeping so please leave," said Jamie.

Bella forced herself to lift her body into a sitting position on the sofa. She rubbed her eyes and checked her watch. She had only dozed off for ten minutes, but it felt like forever. Jamie and Liz approached, and they looked at each other.

"Hey, Bella. Claudia is here. She wants to speak to you," Liz said. "I tried to get rid of her but she won't leave."

Bella nodded. "That's fine. Bring her inside."

She took in the sight of the dishevelled Claudia before her. Her face looked gaunt, and her body was shaking. Either she had something to hide or she was as freaked out as Bella was about the entire situation from last night.

Claudia sat opposite her on the armchair while Liz and Jamie sat on either side of her on the couch. "I'm sorry about last night but I wasn't involved. The police questioned me for hours but I didn't do anything."

Bella watched her closely. She looked convincing. "But you came over to my house and stole my necklace."

Claudia winced, her face blank. "What are you talking about? I never came here and I already told you that I didn't steal your damn necklace."

Liz put up a hand. "Settle down."

Jamie intervened. "You do have a grudge against Bella. Admit it."

Claudia shook her head. "I had nothing to do with last night or any of those other things they accused me of. The vandalism, the necklace, and those toxic text messages. None of it was me."

Bella's eyes darkened. "But the detective had some kind of lead, which was why he questioned me about you last night. He was even watching you at the party."

Claudia's face reddened. "I know about that, but it wasn't me. Someone is setting me up. We might've had our differences, Bella, but I would never hurt you this way."

Silence filled the room until the doorbell rang again. Liz answered it.

Marco walked in without his partner. "How are you feeling?"

She winced in pain. "I'll live."

He angled his head and stood in his spot. "Ladies. This has to be between Bella and the police. Can we please have the room?"

"No, I don't mind if they listen in, detective. Please let them be here."

He nodded. "We spoke to the two men who were at the party last night. One of them admitted to being an accomplice. He got paid to distract you, Liz. The other man admitted to someone making contact over the phone. The voice was disguised so he couldn't tell me the gender. Whoever it was had offered him a lot of money to do what he did."

Liz paled and turned to Bella. "I had a feeling that guy I met was dodgy. Then I remembered seeing them together earlier and decided to come find you. That's when Penny told me you had gone to the bathroom and thank God I arrived when I did. Or he would've..."

Bella drew back. "Thanks again, Liz."

Marco continued. "The perpetrator from last night bought this particular drug to induce paralysis so he could control you. He was ordered to rape you." He fixated on Bella. "We believe this stalker's extremely dangerous. It doesn't appear that these men were involved in the stalking but were in it for quick cash. We weren't able to trace anything on the man's phone. The stalker must have used a burner phone."

Bella was sick to the stomach. Her friends watched her with sympathy in their eyes. Marco's gaze was serious and dark.

Claudia said, "And what about me?"

Marco clasped his hands together and squared his shoulders. "We don't believe you're a person of interest any longer. We have reason to believe you might have been set up. I don't know why you've been targeted but this stalker must know your history with Bella. The fact that you've had conflict and disagreements. I will keep you in the loop when I can, Bella."

Claudia's eyes brightened as she sighed with relief. She stared at Bella as if she felt a tad of empathy towards her. Did she suddenly have a soul?

The dank smell of the basement was familiar, almost exciting. The windowless room kept delicious secrets. Tools of the art that included medical equipment sat on a stark, steel tray. A woman, the latest, stared, helpless. Eyes wide and shaking, her mouth was stuffed with a piece of dirty fabric. She was naked, covered by beautiful wounds made by cigarette burns and knife slices.

Grabbing the scalpel and cutting across her right wrist and then the left one created a sigh of euphoria. Chuckling, as the woman's cries were muffled through the fabric. Her body quivering like beautiful music. The stirrups secured her legs, and a thick rope was tied around her chest. She wasn't going anywhere. The red blood poured out. "Oh, the joy of your slow death." She closed her eyes. "No, no, no. You are going to stay awake and feel the pain of your death." Slapping her hard across the face, her eyes were forced open. The serrated knife glistened in the tray. It cut easily across her carotid artery. All the life flowed out of her. She was gone. Rejuvenated by adrenaline. "So goddam horny." Touching private parts, pleasuring. All was right with the world. Or almost. All traces of this bitch had to be gone. "Now, back to business. I have to clean up this mess."

Chapter Thirty-Eight

A REVELATION

Fear filled Bella as she sat on a towel looking out at the ocean, the sea breeze feather–light on her cheeks. She prodded her toes in the sand and played with the fine granules as she poured them from one hand to another. The warm sun kissed the skin left exposed by her white singlet top and black shorts. Liz lay beside her with eyes closed, no doubt enjoying the quiet and the sun on her bare back. She wore a bikini top and short jean skirt.

Children in the water threw a plastic ball to one another while a man dived nearby, swimming to a floating raft further out in the water. Beachgoers lazed on towels, walked along the shore picking up shells, and swam over the cycles of shallow waves.

Claudia was no longer a suspect. It had been easier when Bella thought she knew her stalker. Now, an unknown stalker felt much worse.

It was almost summer. She had no family to share the heat with nor the upcoming Christmas holiday. It was always a hard time as she contemplated those she had lost.

Liz's phone buzzed from her bag. She rose from the towel and picked it up. "Hi Jamie. What's up?" She wrinkled her brow. "Sure. We'll be there, but what's this about?" Her face paled. Something was terribly wrong. She ended the call and faced Bella. "We have to meet Jamie at home. She's had some news, but wouldn't tell me over the phone. She was crying horribly. Let's go."

Bella nodded. Without wasting time, they trudged over the sand and headed to Bella's car parked on the main road of Williamstown. She wondered what had happened to Jamie. Maybe it had something to do with her wealthy parents or something about work. She placed her bets on Jamie's father with whom she'd met a few times but never got a good vibe from. There was something about the way he always appeared scattered, uninterested, and distracted, like he didn't want to be around people. Her mother was the opposite and spread a glow of warmth and love. Bella hoped Jamie's family was okay.

Bella sat inside Jamie's open-plan kitchen, her hands touching the silky-smooth table runner. She waited for her friend to come out of the bathroom. Liz was with her. Jamie had been vomiting and Bella wondered if Jamie was pregnant. She wasn't dating anyone, as far as Bella knew.

Jamie and Liz came back into the kitchen and sat across from Bella. She pinched her skin at the throat when scanning Jamie's dazed expression. Dark circles set under her eyes and her hair was unwashed. She looked smaller. Whatever happened had obviously affected her. Jamie never looked so dishevelled.

Liz stroked Jamie's hand. "Can you please tell us what's hurting you, Jamie? We're here for you."

Bella leaned forward. "Whatever it is, Jamie, we'll get through it together."

Jamie shook her head, fighting back tears. "I am sorry, Bella. After what you are enduring, I feel so selfish to be worrying about me."

"It's okay. Everyone has their own pain. What's the problem? Is it your family?"

She shook her head. "Of course not. If they had a problem, I am almost certain my dad would pay someone off." Liz looked at Bella, sharing concern. Jamie took a deep breath as her whole upper body shook. She averted her eyes. "Martha's dead."

Bella's hand flew to her chest and her mouth fell open. A heaviness settled in her stomach and tears soaked her cheeks. This couldn't be happening. Surely, she didn't hear correctly. "What?"

Jamie shed more tears and wiped them away. "She was stabbed." Bella flinched. "As if killing is not bad enough, the poor girl was tortured too."

"Oh my God, Jamie. I am so sorry," said Bella.

Liz remained silent.

Jamie's body shook, tears falling heavily down her sunken, pale cheeks. Without words, they consoled each other in silence with bowed heads, each feeling their own pain and shock. Bella wrapped her arms around Jamie, and Liz buried her face in her hands.

Jamie shifted. "I spoke to George, who had to identify her body. It was almost unrecognisable. He was beside himself." She exhaled. "George told me something strange, though."

"What?" Liz suddenly seemed to have recovered from the shock.

"She had these words marked in paint on her body." Jamie briefly closed her eyes. "It said, 'You've Been Marked.'"

Bella clutched at her throat and couldn't speak. The exact same words written in paint on Bridget's body. The exact same words written on her building.

Liz held Bella's hand. "Are you okay?"

Bella's eyes glazed. "It's just a bit of a shock, but I'll be okay." She turned to Jamie who cowered and visibly trembled. Putting her thoughts aside, she pulled Jamie up. "Come on, I'm taking you to bed. Sleep and rest are what you need, and we'll be here with you."

"I'll be fine. Stop fussing." Her eyelids drooped.

"No, you're not. It's okay to mourn, Jamie." Bella pushed Jamie into bed, tucking the blankets up high. She sat on the edge of her bed, stroking her hair. "It's okay. Everything will be all right, Jamie." She stayed glued to the bed until Jamie closed her eyes.

Bella met with Liz back in the kitchen. "Jamie and Martha were close. She's dealing with a lot right now."

Liz nodded. "I know."

The thought that someone she cared about died made her want to run. Bella's stomach was rock hard when she ran into the bathroom to be sick.

Chapter Thirty-Nine

SAYING GOODBYE

Bella strolled along the uneven, cracked concrete, looking up at the grey-black structure of St Mary's Church with its steeple, narrow windows, and surrounding bollards. The glare of the sun penetrated her retinas, almost blinding her, and the wind blew gently like a summer's breeze in springtime.

She stepped into the church, nauseous, and grabbed a funeral booklet from a young skinny girl standing by the door. The quiet whispers of the mourners made the grief for Martha real and sad. Smiling at the girl, she made her way towards Liz who was seated at the back of the church. Jamie sat close to the front, talking to a towering man. Bella assumed the man was George, Martha's husband.

Sitting on the hard bench, Bella greeted Liz. "How's Jamie doing?"

Liz shrugged. "Not well. They couldn't even have a rosary or viewing because of the bad shape of her body. That poor woman." A single tear fell down Liz's gaunt cheek.

"Are you okay, Liz?"

Liz nodded, then turned away. Something was definitely wrong. It seemed to be more than about Martha, but Bella didn't pry.

Bella didn't want to imagine the immeasurable suffering that poor Martha had gone through. Whoever did this didn't deserve to walk the Earth, and she hoped the police would find the perpetrator soon.

A gospel song resounded in the church. Some people sang with the words while others whispered or sat numbly in their seats. The priest stood stiffly at the altar, adjusting his microphone, waiting for the music to end. He eyed the parishioners with curiosity and then welcomed everyone.

Bella felt a tap on her shoulder and turned around.

Marco sat behind her. "I'm sorry for your loss, Bella," he whispered.

"Thanks." Facing the priest again, Bella's quaking hands calmed with the sense of security Marco brought with him. It was nice of him to come.

She remembered from her dabbling in criminology that some killers liked to be involved in the mourning process of their victim and the investigation. The killer could be here somewhere. She tried not to look around, twisting her hands together. She had started shaking again. *That's why Marco is here. He's looking for the killer.*

The priest's sermon was real, honest, and heartfelt. Martha's husband, George recited the eulogy, and a few family members did readings. The looks on their faces tugged at her heart. She couldn't imagine what it would be like to have one of your family members murdered.

At the end of the procession, the casket was carried out of the church and placed in the hearse. She made her way outside into the warm breeze with Liz and Marco to give their condolences to George and Martha's family. Marco's eyes roamed, as if searching for the killer.

In the far distance, standing near the bollards was Jackson. He stood awkwardly and stared out at the guests with a solemn expression. *What in hell is he doing here? Unless...* No, she was being ridiculous and letting her imagination get the better of her. He probably knew Martha somehow, then when he saw Bella, he didn't want to upset her and stayed back.

Marco approached her as the guests were leaving for the burial. "Did you notice Jackson over there?"

Bella nodded. "Why is he here?"

He squinted. "I plan to find out, but I'll hang about and not create a scene. I'll approach him once the guests have left. Hopefully, he'll still be here."

"Do you have a reason to question him?"

"No, but a little informal chit chat isn't out of the question. He doesn't need to respond, but hopefully, he will."

Jamie and Liz approached Bella. She wrapped her arms around Jamie. "I'm so sorry for your loss, Jamie. She was an amazing person."

Jamie rubbed her eyes, her hands visibly shivering. "I still cannot believe she is gone. Who would do this to her? A monster that is not of this Earth, that is who. I will never process this. Never."

Bella held on to Jamie's hand and again wondered if Jackson had anything to do with this. She turned to Jamie. "Do you know if Martha had any male friends?"

Jamie tilted her head. "No, I don't think so. Why?"

Marco headed towards Jackson.

"No reason. Let's go to the burial," said Bella.

Heads down and shoulders slouched, the three friends walked towards the road and waved goodbye to Marco, who was standing, cross-armed near Jackson. Her chest tightened when Jackson spotted her, his eyes remaining glued to hers. He looked guilty but maybe only for the way he'd treated her.

Chapter Forty

SPEAKING ENGAGEMENT

Bella stood in front of the Year 9 class, waving her hands about. She clicked the light pro and, on the screen, appeared a number of scenarios that demonstrated bullying and cyberbullying behaviours. Young students put up their hands and explained how similar situations had occurred to them. The female teacher, Sherry Martin, who had not been there when she attended this school, sat on the side and watched. She was an older woman with grey hair tied up in a bun.

Bella was happy to oblige her old school principal's request for this presentation as she'd had both the experience and training in this specialised area.

The windows let in a bit of glare. The teacher shut the blinds and gestured for students to be quiet and remain in their seats. A few of them were chewing gum, others fixed their gazes on her, and still others whispered to their fellow classmates, nodding in her direction. She suppressed any paranoid ideas because she knew these students could be talking about anything except her.

The air in the classroom was stifling. The familiar setting summoned flashbacks. She remembered how Bridget had sat behind her and whispered, "You've Been Marked." Someone obviously knew the words Bridget had used, unless Bridget had risen from the dead. She returned to the present and cleared her throat. She could do this. The past was the past.

After discussing possible reasons for bullying, Bella explained further. "Not only should you seek help if you're being bullied, but it's important to recognise the signs from any of your friends who are being bullied." She let that sink in. "You might see your friend appear nervous or anxious, losing interest in talking to you. They might not sleep or eat. They might have scratches or bruises on their body. You might notice a change in their behaviour." Interested eyes remained on her. "If any of these things happen, please talk to your teacher who can follow up with the student."

A buxom female student with piercings over her nose and ears, said, "But isn't that tattling, Miss?"

Bella shook her head. "No, you'd be reporting when you realise your friend is harming themselves or others. Tattling is when you want to get someone else in trouble, and this isn't the case here. You all have to stand up for each other."

She spoke about cyberbullying and strategies.

A female student put up her hand. "Miss, have you ever been bullied?"

Bella winced but fought back her nerves. "I have, but I got through it."

"And what did you do? Did you tell your parents?"

Bella gave her a quick glance and breathed deeply. She should've planned for these kinds of questions, but she had to remain professional in front of these students. She couldn't let her guard down. "I didn't, but I realised years later, I should have spoken up. We all need to ask for help. You need support or someone you can talk to. I have these handouts that explain further about what you can do, including contacting the police for more serious cases, or finding ways to block someone online. Remember, that cyber bullying is serious and just as damaging. It's a permanent form of communication that sticks around and exposes you to many other people. It has serious consequences." She gave out the handouts. Bella's hands shook as she circled the room, forcing a smile. Some of the girls watched her with curiosity, and she wondered if they picked up on her nerves.

Maybe she should've chosen a different topic, but the principal was adamant on this area, given the history of bullying at this school.

The students asked a few more questions before the end of the session. They applauded politely.

As they ambled out of the classroom, Bella gathered her documents and turned off the equipment. She thanked Sherry and headed towards the principal's office. Knocking on the door, she smiled at the new principal, Susan, who hadn't been her principal eleven years ago. She replaced the old one who had avoided tackling bullying behaviour at the school.

"Take a seat, Bella. It's great to have you back after all these years. I've heard a bit about you from your old teachers," Susan said. She sported grey strands of hair at her temples and the remaining brown hair was tied up in a loose ponytail. Wrinkles over her face and underneath her eyes showed her age.

"Thanks, Susan. I enjoyed the presentation. The students were open to the topic."

She nodded. "I imagine they would be, considering how it was when I took over. I have heard from one of the older teachers here who knew you. She mentioned how you'd been bullied all those years ago. I'm sorry we couldn't offer you more help. Is that why you left the school after Year 10?"

Bella wished she could steer clear of this subject, but it was to be expected, considering the topic for today. *I can do this. I've survived worse than this.* "I had family issues that forced me to leave the school." She could never tell Susan that the real reason she left was due to her father's trouble with the law. He had wanted to make a fresh start in a new area where nobody knew their business, but he was a criminal inside and out. She remembered how he'd minimized his crime by saying how his aggression was a colleague's fault. He explained that the co-worker should've kept his opinions to himself when her father had been his manager. How laughable, considering her father lacked control of his anger, lashing out both physically and verbally. He'd got sacked from multiple jobs and was charged for assault on more than a few occasions. If he didn't have a dodgy lawyer friend, he would've been incarcerated but he always managed to come out on top.

The principal didn't look convinced as she fixed her gaze on Bella. "Well, I'll be calling you for further presentations. Is that okay?"

Bella nodded. "Of course. I'd be happy to help further."

She left and wondered if the next time around, she'd feel more relaxed.

Chapter Forty-One

THE INTERVIEWS

As Marco took wide strides towards the principal's office inside the school building with Tim, he spotted Bella. Heat radiated through his chest and his hands tingled. *God, she was gorgeous, particularly when she blushed like that.*

"Detectives. What are you doing here?"

Marco suppressed a smile. "We're here on official police business, Bella."

"I see." Her eyes remained glued to his until the spell was broken.

Tim intervened. "Ms Carismo. We'll be seeing you."

Marco nodded in her direction. "We'll be in touch."

"No worries," said Bella who rushed off without a second glance towards the exit. His adrenaline lifted. He waved away the heat from his face and regained his breath.

Brushing away erotic thoughts, they eventually reached the principal's office and knocked on her door.

After introductions, and sitting across from Susan, Marco asked questions about Bridget. "We need whatever information you can provide about Bridget." Susan dug into her files and scanned through them. "Reading some old school files, I discovered that Bridget was one of the main bullies, along with one of her friends, Margaret. She had another friend who stood back from the bullying." She shifted back to her seat. "Bridget was suspended while doing Year 12 as we found out she'd been bullying others too."

"We need a list of those names."

Susan rested an elbow on her desk. "Of course, detective." She started writing out a list on a note pad then handed it to Marco.

Tim asked, "Do you have details of Bridget's behaviour back then?"

Susan gazed past him, placing a finger across her cheek. "She was manipulating these girls. It was so tragic."

Marco angled his head. "What do you mean manipulating them? In what way?"

Susan drew a hand through her grey-streaked brown hair. "Well, one of the teachers reported that Bridget had orchestrated an event whereby a girl's boyfriend was drugged and put in bed with one of

Bridget's friends. After the misunderstanding, the couple made up, but it took a lot of investigating, questioning, and understanding. It was a right mess." She shook her head. "But nothing like that was reported back then."

"What were their names?" Marco asked.

Susan wrote down more names on a note pad. Her eyes roamed. "A teacher by the name of Sherry Martin knew Bridget back then. She tried to help the young girl but struggled. Sherry's won a few awards for her work as a teacher, so she was heartbroken when Bridget wasn't ready for change. She does a lot for the school and has helped a lot of other students."

"Did Sherry know an old student by the name of Bella Carismo?"

Susan smiled. "Oh, I just spoke to Bella earlier. She ran a presentation about bullying to Sherry's class." She leaned forward. "Sherry started here a year after Bella left our school."

Marco shifted his posture. "Would we be able to speak to her?"

Susan nodded. "She's in class now, but I can get her to meet you in one of the rooms near the staffroom. I'll show you to the room. I'm sure she won't mind speaking to you about Dawn or Bridget."

Marco rose. "Great. Thank you." Tim followed him as they were led outside.

Marco and Tim sat on a red sunken couch in the empty classroom. The small room was filled with grey, padded chairs around long timber tables, bookshelves, varnished overhead cupboards, and large windows that had a view of the schoolyard.

Sherry walked up to them. "The principal mentioned you wanted to see me."

Marco got up, and Tim did the same. "Yes, we're from homicide. I'm Detective Senior Constable Marco Petrazini and this is Detective Senior Constable Tim Wittens." They shook hands. "We'd like to talk to you about Bridget Mardot. We're investigating her death."

Sherry frowned and squeezed her hands. "Yes, I heard about that. Tragic." Her eyes misted, then pulled up a chair and sat opposite. "What would you like to know, detectives?"

Tim added, "We spoke to the principal, and she mentioned you filing an incident report on Bridget. We thought you might have information about that." They waited as the woman turned her eyes past them as if recalling the past.

Her eyes glazed. "Yes, I did. Bridget was a bad seed. I honestly don't know how she wasn't expelled from the school." She took a deep breath. "I take it her past caught up with her present somehow." She scrutinised them. "One of Bella's friends, Dawn, eventually spoke to me about Bridget bullying her. You see, Bridget had slept with a boy that Dawn liked. It hurt her terribly. Bridget was also in the habit of beating her up and putting her down on a daily basis. Hence, why she was suspended."

"Was this Dawn's boyfriend?"

"No, only someone she liked. Bridget was that way inclined. Always taking things away from that poor girl. Dawn confided in me about being bisexual too. She had a girlfriend in Year 12, and Bridget taunted her about that too. Bridget said a great many things against Bella to Dawn, and I think Dawn didn't know what to believe about Bella. She was a strong influence and could manipulate anyone."

"And do you know had badly she bullied Bella?" asked Tim.

"From what Dawn told me, she'd seen Bridget bully Bella several times. From what I heard from other students, Bella had been harassed by Bridget for years. She never told anyone. I don't know why she kept the bullying to herself. Dawn happened to see Bridget physically hurt Bella in the bathroom twice, and one time Dawn stood up to her. Later, Dawn was violated even further for standing up to Bridget. As far as I know, Bridget had never bullied their friend, June."

"Do you know the whereabouts of Dawn? We've had trouble locating her."

Sherry shook her head. "No, sorry detectives." She sighed. "Poor June died so she's out of the picture."

Marco felt sick in the stomach, wondering how much more hell Bella had been through.

Sherry drew a wrinkly hand through her hair, fixing her gaze on Marco. "Dawn mentioned something else. I could tell something was wrong in class, so I questioned her afterwards. She mentioned being betrayed by a friend, but she refused to tell me who it was, even after I insisted. This friend had been spilling out false information to her parents about Dawn sleeping around with both girls and boys in school. Apparently, this friend had also spread rumours about her sexuality. Dawn was beside herself with grief at having thought her friend was on her side. Bridget told her about these rumours."

Tim asked, "Do you believe this friend was Bella?"

"I don't know. Most likely it was Bella as Bridget didn't like her, and she never bullied June. Dawn didn't have other friends." She paused. "Bridget could be very persuasive. Dawn even showed me how the text message around the school came from this particular mobile number. It was not long after she left."

Marco clenched his hands. "She must've masked her phone number to make her think it was Bella."

She waved her hand away. "Oh, I know that. Bridget was cleverly evil in many ways and seemed to have gone to a lot of effort to turn Dawn against this friend. She was pretty tech savvy too. Quite scary how intelligent Bridget was."

What Dawn must've thought about Bella. She must've thought their whole four-year friendship had been a lie.

"I tried to get Bridget expelled, but her parents had money and wealth so could buy their way into anything."

Marco pondered this new information about Bridget, who kept sounding worse by the minute.

Chapter Forty-Two

FRIGHTFUL NEWS

A few days later, Bella squeezed her knuckles, exploring the whiteness of her skin, deeply engrossed in the wavy patterns across her hands and the dryness of her skin. Her stomach did somersaults as she shifted her posture and waited for Marco at the pizza restaurant. He'd offered to buy her lunch this Saturday morning to give her news. She wondered whether he'd had a new lead or if something sinister had occurred. Whatever it was, she was a bundle of nerves, with conflicting emotions about seeing Marco again.

She thought about his gentle hands, the tender way he'd held her when they danced at the masquerade party, the way his taut, tanned muscles caused a flutter in her heart, and the tingles she'd felt when he touched her even lightly. Those lips enticed her to kiss him, and she wanted his hands to touch her all over. Closing her eyes, she could hear his voice in her mind, and picture the masculine curves and strength of his body.

Sitting on the hard-backed chair, Bella imagined the darkness of the restaurant creating a romantic ambience. Couples gazed into each other's eyes and held each other's hands around her. She shook her head, being silly. Maybe she needed to start dating again. If she could find someone who was more in her league and not working her case, she'd be able to forget about Marco. He wasn't right for her in many ways.

She turned her head towards the door as Marco entered, wearing a tight-fitted white shirt with rolled-up sleeves and brown pleated plants. His hair was ruffled, probably due to the wind. He beamed at the sight of her.

"Hey, Bella. Sorry I'm late. I had to follow-up on a few things regarding this case." He sat down, ushering over the waiter. "I'm famished. Is it okay if we eat before I give you the news? I don't want to spoil your appetite."

Bella became curious, tilting her head. "What's this about?"

"All in good time. I'd like to have a nice drink first. I hope you don't mind meeting here for lunch?"

Bella touched her neck. "No, that's fine."

The waiter came over and wrote down their orders of pizza and drinks. Once he left, Marco rubbed his hands and stared into her eyes without saying anything. Bella looked away, an awkward tension in the air. She wished he'd say something as she was suddenly tongue-tied. Her hands chilled.

When the waiter returned with their drinks—a glass of Moscato for Bella and a glass of mineral water for Marco—she quickly drank half of it, letting the lightness of the wine warm her.

"How are you feeling after the funeral?"

"I'm okay, but I can't say the same for Jamie. She was closer to Martha than I was. It's really hit her hard. She's taken time off work and has gone to stay with her parents for a week. She's still in shock."

Marco nodded. "I can't imagine losing a close friend like that. It'll take time and the support of her loved ones."

"I know, and we're there for her, but I can't shake this uneasy feeling that things will get worse before they get better."

Marco squinted. "Why? Has something else happened?"

"No, my stalker's been quiet, and I haven't seen Jackson around. But that doesn't mean I won't see him one of these days."

"We're keeping an eye on him, don't worry."

"Hmm," Bella said.

The fresh herb smell of pizza filled her senses when the waiter brought the two trays of it and settled them on the table. They dug into their respective pizzas, the silence welcome as they devoured and sipped their drinks.

Once they finished eating, Marco frowned and faced Bella. "I think there's a pattern to these crimes."

Bella gasped. "What are you talking about?"

"We discovered that one of Bridget's friends got murdered a few years back in a different state. The way it was staged fits the exact crimes of both Martha and Bridget. We're possibly looking at a cross-investigation now." Bella felt goose bumps over her body, frozen in time. She blinked a few times, and whether it was the wine or not, the restaurant was spinning around her. "Are you okay?"

His voice sounded far, but Bella steeled herself. "Are we looking at a serial killer?"

Marco nodded. "It certainly looks that way. What bothers me is the connection these murders have to you. You were friends with Martha and well-acquainted with Bridget and her friend. I don't know what the connection is apart from that." He exhaled. "What is the reasoning behind these murders? I haven't figured that out yet."

Her throat burned. "Do you think it might be Jackson?"

Marco shrugged. "I'm trying to dig into his history. I haven't yet found any connection between him and these women." He shifted. "I'd like to ask you about Bridget's friend, Margaret."

"I can answer any questions you have about Bridget's friend, but I didn't know her that well. All I know is her following Bridget's lead, but had more of a conscience."

Marco swallowed. "We're following a few lines of enquiry. Don't worry, we'll catch this person." His eyes darkened. "You'll need to go into a bit more about your past, Bella. There has to be something we're missing here."

She sat stock-still, not wanting to dig into her past. Whoever did this obviously hated women. "Can you please look into Jackson first, and see whether he's a suspect?"

Marco gave her a reassuring smile. "We're already doing that but going into your past might offer us a clue, a lead, perhaps." He peered into his drink and took a sip. "We can't wait on this for too long. Time is an issue, and this person might escalate towards you."

Bella shrugged. "I can take care of myself, detective."

"No doubt, but we are dealing with a sociopathic killer here, and I am deeply worried. I...I...don't want...I would never forgive myself if....something....something happened to you." His face reddened.

Bella's heart warmed and she smiled to herself. This was crazy. A serial killer was lurking in her life, and she was having erotic thoughts and feelings about a detective. How crazy was that? She was in fear for her life but found herself mesmerised by the man across from her. He made her feel safe. Why did it have to be so wrong because of his professional connection to her?

He faced her again. "Like I said, time's of the essence, and it's looking like you need to tell us more about your past."

Oh, Christ...

Bella took an evening stroll in the park across from her work building. She'd had a late client and wasn't ready to go home yet, needing to gather her thoughts about Marco. He wanted to know about her past, and she cringed at the idea. She knew it could possibly provide a lead, but she struggled to go there. All this time, she had survived and managed to deal with her trauma. Why go there again?

Kicking scattered leaves across the ground, Bella watched passersby walk hurriedly through the park. She stood by a tree and kept her head down, calming her thoughts. When she looked up at her surroundings, the park had become eerily quiet, and the sun was slowly going down. She shouldn't have worked until 8:30 p.m., but she sometimes had to accommodate clients who worked late. The sounds of crickets, whispering trees, and a plane flying overhead gave her comfort. In spite of that, she hurriedly walked back towards the road where her car was parked. She became uneasy and felt alone. Looking around, all was quiet. Footsteps suddenly sounded behind her. She turned, but no-one was in this part of the park. A few more metres and she'd be at her car. Taking a breath, Bella shook her head. Her silly imagination was playing tricks on her again. Reaching for her car's remote in her handbag, she felt a bang against the back of her head and a sharp pain. Her wrist was wrenched backwards. Then darkness.

Chapter Forty-Three

A HOSPITAL VISIT

Bella roused from her sleep, hearing a soft breath nearby. She slowly opened her eyes. White, crisp sheets wrapped around her legs. A sharp headache penetrated down into her neck muscles and her body felt like lead. Her right wrist was bandaged but the stabbing pain caused her to wince. *What the hell!* Looking around, a vase of flowers sat by her bedside and a large window let in glaring sunlight. She was in a hospital. The smell of disinfectant and footsteps in the distance was further evidence she wasn't at home. Was she dreaming?

A short woman carrying a stethoscope around her neck waltzed in with a warm smile. She had the muscles of a weightlifter. Taking a clipboard from the edge of the bed, she approached Bella. "How are you doing, honey?"

"Not great." She sighed. "Why am I here?"

"You were assaulted, love. A passerby saw you lying in the park and called the ambulance. You're very lucky the cuts on your wrist weren't worse. You lost a bit of blood. Very lucky, indeed. I'll check your blood pressure and temperature." The nurse gave her a reassuring smile. "All good, love. Is there anything you need?"

She fought back the heaviness in her chest. "No, I'm fine, thank you."

The nurse beamed, then scurried out of the ward.

Peering through the window, the smell of musky aftershave penetrated her nostrils. As she turned to the doorway, her heartbeat sped up. Inhaling deeply, she managed a smile as Marco returned it.

"How are you feeling?"

Bella shrugged. "A bit sore, but I'll be fine."

He squinted. "Listen, I think we need to talk about something." He took out his phone and put it close to Bella's face. "This note was left at the scene. The paramedics found it tucked into your hand."

Bella stared at the screen, drawing back in horror at the typed message: *The clock is ticking. Tick-tock-tick-tock.* "What were you doing in the park alone?"

"I had a late client and was too wound up to go home. A few people were walking through the park. I thought it was safe. Then suddenly I was alone." Marco clenched his jaw. "As I said, I felt safe in the beginning."

"I wish you hadn't gone to the park alone, Bella. After what we discussed about you being in danger. Something worse could've happened to you."

"I'm sorry." The look in his eyes ran beyond professional duty. "I need you to locate my old friend, Dawn."

Marco held his chin with his hand. "I've had an officer look into Dawn, but so far we haven't been able to find anything. I'll look deeper and get back to you." He sat in the chair opposite and leaned forward. "I'm wondering if the stalker thought you were investigating at the school rather than giving a presentation to the students. They might've thought you were fishing around."

She nodded. "It's possible, but you guys were the ones investigating, not me."

"Have faith in us, Bella. We have a few leads we need to follow, but I need something from you. Basically, what I mentioned the last time we spoke."

Bella's chest tingled. "What is it?" But she already knew the answer.

"I need you to tell me everything you remember about your friends, your family history, and the bullying that went on at school. We got information from the teacher and principal, but I need your story, your perspective. This is crucial to our investigation, Bella. Can you do that?"

She wanted to vomit. "I know you're right, but..."

Marco sighed. "The threat level has just risen to imply there's a time factor here. I'd say that counts for something. I strongly believe there's a link from your past now. Whatever it is, no matter how trivial, might mean something. You need to share everything that might progress this investigation. There are high stakes here."

Bella briefly closed her eyes, wanting to shut out the world. She had to tell Marco about the atrocities that had occurred both at home and at school. This killer had raised the stakes, so she had no choice but to tell him everything.

Chapter Forty-Four

CONFIDANTE

Bella shifted her weight in the hospital bed as Marco pressed his lips together, waiting for her to begin. The reassuring smile on his face and relaxed posture made her feel safe. Taking a deep breath, she peered into her hands and started.

Bella was sixteen, in the prime of her life, when she was walking outside her class during lunch break. She usually met her friends, Dawn and June, near the oval when it was the warm season. As she stepped onto the asphalt, hearing the crunching sound underneath her feet, a shove from behind propelled her forward onto the ground. She grazed her chin and cheeks, the pain stopping her from rising instantly. Moaning, she turned and tried to get up. A foot kicked her in the back.

"You bitch. You were supposed to help me with my assignment but instead you got me a measly D grade. My parents are angry with me because I didn't get a damn A. All because of you."

Bella rose and wiped the stones off her body, cringing under the steely gaze of Bridget, her nemesis and bully. "I practically wrote the assignment for you, but something happened the day I worked on it. My parents..."

"Your parents what, bitch?"

"Nothing. I'm sorry. I'll do better next time."

She wouldn't tell Bridget the truth; her father belted her after she failed to get home on time from her volunteer role, working with disabled clients. She'd stopped for a milkshake with a fellow volunteer, and her father had punished her. Over that weekend, she'd had little time to complete Bridget's assignment because she'd been further punished with errands for both her parents. Her mother was always drunk. On the rare occasion she was sober she was okay, but she never stood up to her own husband. He treated his wife like dirt too, and she coped by drinking.

Bridget shook her head. "Not good enough." She turned to her friend standing beside her. "Grab her. Take her to the toilets."

Bella gasped, prickles of fear making her skin crawl. She watched passersby staring but doing nothing. She couldn't see her friends anywhere.

Bridget's friend, Margaret, shoved her into the toilet block. Both Bridget and Margaret stood cross-armed. "Clear off! I'm going to enjoy my alone time with Bella. She needs to understand that I mean business."

Bella stood back against the grimy, vandalised bathroom wall. Her chest was tight, her mouth dry. Tears fell and she wiped them away with a quivering hand.

Bridget approached, her face inches from Bella's. She grimaced, grabbed Bella by the shirt, pulled her forward, and smashed the back of her head into the mirror. The mirror cracked. Blood seeped from the back of Bella's head, her eyes drooping closed. She tried to fight the encroaching darkness. Bridget glared. "You tell anyone about this or about our arrangement, even to your friends, and I'll come by to your house and kill your mother." She smirked. "Looks like we need to get that blood off." Lunging towards Bella, she grabbed Bella by the collar of her uniform, pulled her towards the toilet bowl and pushed her face into it.

She pulled her out and was about to soak her face again when Bella cried, and begged, "No, please, not again. Enough, please!"

Bridget scoffed. "You're a loser and only losers beg." Ignoring her plea, she pushed her head back into the water and Bella shivered and fought for breath until pulling her out. With another shove,

Bridget ran out of the toilet block as soon as other students walked inside.

Later that week, Bridget pulled Bella into an empty classroom, flexing a soft ruler in her hands. She glared at Bella, moving back, then lifted up her right arm and swung the ruler hard across her arms. Cuts and bruises lined her skin. Before Bridget left the room, Dawn spotted them and rushed inside with fire in her eyes. One look at Bella's arms led her to kick Bridget hard in the stomach. Dawn's eyes were fiery and dark, the anger in them a little scary. But surely, anyone who'd been bullied by Bridget deserved to stand up for themselves?

Bella never told any of her friends what was going on over the two years of bullying. Dawn believed it had only happened a few times, but it was a lot more than that.

From her grown-up perspective, Bella had tolerated it, believing she deserved the bullying. It wasn't only about her mother. Now, she knew better.

Bella stopped talking and returned to the present.

Marco's face was white, his eyes filled with sorrow. He held her hand in his and stroked it gently. He was silent for a minute. "I am so sorry for what you went through. I know that Bridget threatened you, but did you ever think about telling your parents or anyone else?"

Bella avoided his eyes. "My father was abusive, and my mother was mostly drunk. She was okay when she wasn't drinking, but Bridget had threatened her. I couldn't take that risk. My mother treated me well enough when she wasn't drunk, but it was my aunt who truly saved me. She's dead now."

Marco nodded, his eyes briefly looking elsewhere. "I'm sorry. You've been through so much pain and loss." He drew closer. "What about your friend, Dawn? Would she be capable of hurting Bridget?"

Bella shrugged. No doubt, Marco would've known from his investigation. "Dawn? I don't know." Her head ached. "You're telling me that whoever killed Bridget is possibly stalking me now? But I was friends with Dawn. I never hurt her in any way, so these revenge killings don't make sense. Even with Martha."

Marco looked past her. "Your parents? Do you see them, or know whether your father would hurt you this way?"

Bella chuckled. "He's not smart enough to do all this. This stalker's organised and smart, obviously knows about my past, and could be looking at framing someone else after Claudia."

"When was the last time you spoke to your other friend, June?"

Bella's heart hurt. "I said goodbye to June after finishing Year 10, as we were moving house. I assume you know that June died from cancer?" He nodded. "Dawn apparently came to visit me at home a few days before we left. My father sent her away after, telling her I didn't want to be friends any longer. That was a lie. He only wanted me to be alone, to continue taunting me. He also told Dawn she was not welcome at the house and to stop contacting me. I didn't know about it until after she'd left. I wasn't home so I never got the chance to see her at the door."

"I'm sorry. That must've been hard."

Bella tilted her head, curious in her thoughts. "If only I got the chance to tell Dawn the truth. She'd know I wasn't lying." Her throat ached. "She always said 'I can tell when you lie.'" She expelled a breath. "For all I know, Dawn could be married now. She was always kind to me and defended me against Bridget. I hope you find her." Marco's eyes darkened. "Let me look deeper into this and get back to you. In the meantime, I want you to stay with one of your friends."

Bella shook her head. "I'll be fine. I'm not letting this person ruin my life like this. I've been scared for far too long and I'm fighting back now. I never fought back then but I am stronger now."

"Well, at least try not to go anywhere on your own. Be vigilant wherever you go."

"Okay. I'll be careful."

A few days later, the person watched and stood, hands on hips as Bella walked with her friends, Liz and Jamie, out of the hospital towards a parked car. Hating hospitals, the person pondered a time that had almost led to a hospital admission.

Legs strapped to a metal plate. "Oh God!" The cuts in the thighs made the pain unbearable. "Bloody kill me now." A hideous figure stood nearby with a missing tooth, dishevelled beard and hairy body that made him look like Big Foot. The man had a mocking smile, ripping off t-shirt buttons while the fabric tied around the wrists dug into the person's skin. The ugly creature pelted hard into the person's chest with a sledge hammer. Bruises festered, with broken bones. The person got through the torture, imagining a soul mate, best friend, and confidante. The person's parents entered, staring at the show. The mother lit up like a shining star, moaning as if aroused. The father kissed her hungrily on the lips, then said, "Stop! Enough punishment. Get your things and leave."

The ugly man grunted in response. He walked out of the room. The parents untied the person, providing freedom from the binds. The person squirmed. The mother looked on with dead eyes.

No emotion. Pulling the person off the metal table, the mother said, "Let this be a lesson to you. If you continue to disobey us, your punishment will get much worse. That nice gentleman is on speed dial. Let this be a warning."

One day, the person vowed to give the parents a fate worse than death.

Chapter Forty-Five

GENTLE HAND

Bella was back at work, a week after being attacked.

She inserted case files into her filing cabinet, the last of her clients done for the day. Mari interrupted Bella as she manoeuvred her body to the desk then turned.

"Hey, Mari. Are you off?"

Her eyes were red and puffy. "I guess I am."

Bella angled her head, curious. "Have you been crying?"

Mari shrugged. "Just boyfriend blues, Bella. Nothing to worry about. I'll get over it."

"I'm sorry. I didn't realise you were seeing someone."

She averted her eyes. "I love the guy and the bastard broke up with me. It might've been for the best, as he was a little possessive." She rubbed her eyes then fiddled. "Anyway, enough about me. You have a good night."

"Are you sure you'll be okay?"

She rubbed her eyes. "Fine. I've been through worse things than a breakup. Don't worry. See you."

"Bye, Mari. I'll see you tomorrow." She watched her sniffle then walk out.

Bella had never seen Mari in such a state, but she was probably better off without a possessive boyfriend. She'd better steer clear of those types of people.

Feeling bad for Mari, she called her back. "Mari, why don't we go out for dinner? You need to eat."

Mari averted her eyes. "I don't know. I'm not that hungry."

Bella moved forward. "You have to keep your strength up. Just let me get my bag." She scurried into her office then returned to Mari. "Let's go for a walk across to the cafe."

Mari nodded, her mind seemingly elsewhere.

The breeze was noticeably cool, and seagulls flew overhead. The cafe was within easy reach of her building. They took a slow walk, crossing the road and dodging passersby who rushed on home, and children playing in the park on the other side.

She wondered what it was like to feel deeply for a man as Mari obviously felt for her ex-boyfriend, but she didn't have the time nor inclination for romance.

Once they reached the cafe, they sat opposite each other and ordered a chicken Caesar salad for Bella and a sirloin steak with vegetables for Mari. Her mood had changed, possibly well enough for an appetite.

"Did you want to talk about your ex?"

She let out a huge breath. "Not really. I need to forget about him." The waiter brought out their drinks, nodding as he left.

Mari sipped her water and almost dropped the glass. "How are things with you after the Jackson fiasco?"

"I'm fine. I decided not to lay charges against him."

Mari knit her brows. "Why not? The guy deserved it after what he put you through. I'm sorry I couldn't help you earlier that day."

Bella swallowed. "No, it's all good. You weren't to know."

Mari's gaze darkened, her hands fiddling with her hair. "Is there something else happening with you? I mean, the vandalism too."

Bella didn't want to worry Mari, so kept things to herself. "Nothing to worry about."

Mari leaned forward. "Has the detective had any leads on the vandal?" Bella looked downward. "Bella? What is it?"

"It's nothing."

Mari pressed her lips together. "Come on, now. I confided in you about my ex, so I'm here to listen. Let me be a friend. I owe you a lot for everything."

Bella's heart softened at Mari's stricken face. "I'm being stalked."

Mari's eyes widened. "Oh, my God!" She placed her hand over her mouth. "I'm so sorry. Was it the vandal doing that? Is that what the police think?"

"No, I think the stalker paid them off." She explained other events and Mari's pale face made her wish she hadn't divulged so much. But the receptionist was easy to talk to and seemed to want to help.

"Mari reached for her hand. "I'm here for you, Bella, and I'm glad I got to know you. You're like a sister to me, and you care about people."

Bella's heart went out to Mari. "You're too generous, and you look out for me. Thanks." Mari beamed, her face turning beetroot red.

Once the waiters brought out their food, Mari's mood had lifted, and Bella knew that taking her mind off her ex-boyfriend would help. Who needed men, anyway?

❧❧❧❧❧❧ ❧❧❧❧❧❧

As Bella and Mari went their separate ways, Bella remembered forgetting her mobile phone at work. She quickly rushed in, retrieved it from her office desk, then locked the door behind her. She walked towards her car at the kerb when she stopped midway. Her breath burst in and out when spotting Jackson near her building.

As she pushed forward and took long steps to her car, he ran towards her. Bella drew back and held up a hand in defence. "What do you want?"

Jackson was carrying a drawstring bag, and she wondered what was in it." Please, Bella. I'm not here to hurt you. I just wanted to apologise for the way I behaved. I'm sorry."

Her body was shaking, but she ignored her nerves. "Why are you really here?"

He knit his brows and stood with his arms crossed. "Listen, that detective told me you were being harassed. He asked me whether I was the one doing it, but I'm not. I came here to give you this." He handed her the drawstring bag and Bella took it, peering inside. It was a long can of something.

"What is this?"

"It's pepper spray."

Bella flinched. She handed back the bag quickly. "Are you mad? This is illegal. How did you even get this?"

"I have my ways, but I got this for your protection. You need to be careful."

Bella winced. "Is that a threat?"

He shook his head. "Of course not. I would never wish you harm. That other day, I don't know what came over me. I get triggered sometimes. I'm somewhere else. I am seeing someone now who is helping me with the past, but I wasn't ready to work on my history with you. I care about you, Bella. Maybe one day we can be more than friends."

She chuckled. "Are you serious?"

The look of pain in his eyes was evident. "I hope that one day you can forgive me, but in the meantime, this pepper spray can help."

"I'm not taking it. You can have it back." She sighed. "Why do you think I need protection?"

He moved closer towards her and stroked her cheek tenderly. "Please use that. It's all you need to know."

She recoiled from him. Bella got the sense he was telling the truth, but she could not offer him more than the benefit of the doubt. "Good luck with your recovery, Jackson." She turned away and entered her car, locking the door. Before she turned on the motor, a sudden bang across her window made her jump. Her heart felt like it had leapt out her chest, thinking it was Jackson. It was Marco. She opened the window.

Marco looked at her with curiosity. "Are you okay?" He crouched down to her level.

"I'm all right."

He squinted in the sunlight. "We've been keeping an eye on Jackson. Did he threaten you, Bella?"

Bella shook her head. "No, he didn't." She explained their conversation.

Marco stared past her. "Do you think he knows something?"

"I think he has a secret, and I wish I knew what it was."

"We'll get to the bottom of it, and will keep watching him. Be careful."

She turned on the motor and had a measure of comfort, knowing that Marco wasn't far away from her building.

Chapter Forty-Six

INTIMATE MOMENT

Bella arrived home the next day, and spotted Marco getting out of his car in front of her house. She waved as she parked her car in the garage and headed to the front, turning to Marco with a smile.

"Hi, Bella. Can I come inside?"

Bella nodded. "Of course."

He followed her into the house, her awareness of his breathing behind her strong as he touched the small of her back.

They sat on the couch side by side,. "Our investigation has led us to Perth. I'll be away for a few days, depending on what we find, so you need to be careful. My partner will be available if you need anything."

She hid her disappointment. "Okay, but I'll be fine."

"You have to be extra careful."

"I will. My friends are around." She clasped her hands together. "What's in Perth?"

"I can't really say." He changed the subject. "I'm glad I caught you. I wanted to check in and let you know of my absence." He looked at his watch, frowning. "You're home late. Did you have a late client?"

"Yes, I have a client who works long hours so I can only see her after seven."

Marco's hands lightly clenched, and he scoffed. "I don't think it's wise you getting home when it's dark. It's riskier getting home later than usual. You could arrange to have one of your friends drive with you."

"I'll be fine, detective."

"I don't care. I want you to be safe, Bella. I...I..." He turned away, a dark expression in his eyes.

Bella's body responded with a racing pulse and an electrical jolt in her legs. She was speechless, imagining all the things she wanted him to say. "You what?"

"Nothing, Bella. Please take precautionary steps and let me do my job." He leaned forward and brushed a strand of hair out of her eyes, biting his lower lip, his eyes staring deeply into her own. He brushed his hand over her face and Bella's skin warmed under his touch. She closed her eyes, savouring the tenderness of his hands. She ached to hold him, kiss him, and touch him, but her body stayed frozen to the spot. Marco arched his back and shifted closer. He picked up her hand and feathered it across his own cheek, eventually pulling back. "Anyway, my partner will keep watch while I'm gone. Please be careful."

Bella pushed down her emotions. "I will, and I hope you find something in Perth."

He nodded, and turned to leave, but then faced her again. "Listen, this is my card with my personal mobile number on it. I don't mind you calling me day or night if something goes wrong and you need to get help quickly. I've got quick and direct access to the local police."

She took the card from his hand. "Thanks."

Marco's eyes darkened. "I'll be in touch in the next day or so to see how you're doing."

When he left, she winced at the thought of him leaving for Perth. This was all too much. She was horribly sad at the idea of being away from Marco. She felt cold without his presence.

❧❧❧❧❧❧ ❧❧❧❧❧❧

After eating dinner, Bella booted up her laptop and searched for Dawn Heartfelt on social media. She started with Twitter but got nothing. Then she clicked into LinkedIn, Instagram, and finally Facebook. She'd found a number of Dawns in Facebook profiles but nothing that matched her friend. Dawn was most likely happily married with children now. She would've hopefully recovered from her bullying days. Love could do that. After all these years, Dawn would have moved on with a new life.

She turned off the laptop and got ready for bed. *I need to set things straight with Dawn. Tell her the truth about Bridget and my father's lies.* She could find Dawn's parents' address. She remembered where she'd lived and had once met her outside her house, but she'd never been inside. Could her parents tell her where Dawn was living now?

Chapter Forty-Seven

PAST INSIGHT

Bella sat in her kitchen, pondering why Marco went interstate. What was in Perth?

She stared into her cup of tea, watching the steam hovering in the air, and took a sip. Suddenly realising the reason, she gasped. Jackson mentioned coming from Perth before settling in Melbourne. Was that why Marco went to Perth? Did he have people to speak to about Jackson's past?

When her mobile phone rang, she looked at the screen and a tingle flowed in her fingers. *Marco*. She picked up the phone. "Hi, Marco. How's Perth?"

"Not very good. A bit of a dead-end actually."

"Are you there because of Jackson?" Silence. "Marco? Can you tell me anything about the investigation?"

She heard a sigh over the phone. "Listen, I don't want you getting involved in this. This stalker is highly dangerous. Please believe we're following every path and are getting close. We're doing everything we can to catch him."

"I know you've got surveillance on me, so I'll be fine." She heard him grunt. "Why can't you tell me if this is about Jackson? He's from Perth."

"I want you to behave and stay safe. We're a bit short-staffed so the surveillance will only be temporary."

"I appreciate the help, but I'm a big girl and can take care of myself."

"Listen, about the other day. I should apologise again, but I...care about you, Bella. More than you know. When I get back, I'd like us to talk. Maybe after this case is over... things can be different."

Her heart burned with desire. Hearing his voice created a yearning for him, but she couldn't focus on that now. She wanted this stalker caught. "Sure, we can talk. When are you getting back?"

"In about three days. I'll see you then, and please take care."

Bella's stomach turned. "Okay."

Later that day, Bella stepped into her car and headed over to Dawn's old house. This surely didn't count as investigating. Bella was only looking up an old friend.

All those years ago, came rushing back as she stared up at the house.

Dawn had lived in Williamstown, not far from the beach and close to Bella's old home. As she passed by reserves, storefront shops, and rickety-looking houses, she finally found Dawn's house. The house looked like it had been renovated. Even the front garden looked fresh and new. She was sure this was the number of the house, but it looked so different. Had they demolished the old house and built a new one? This house was a cottage-style free-standing house featuring timber-framed windows with the blinds drawn and a worn-out brick veneer. Two towering trees and foliage covered parts of the window, and a freshly paved concrete path looked only a few years old. Were her parents still living here and had decided to renovate?

She walked out of the car and opened the creaking gate, an uneasy feeling settling over her as she walked along the path towards the house. It would be great to see her old friend as they had a lot to catch up on and resolve. Dawn would understand.

Bella rang the doorbell. She waited for a few minutes before hearing the shuffling of feet, and a woman's voice, saying, "I'm coming." She wondered if the woman was Dawn's mother, but the voice sounded old.

The door swung open and a short, petite woman with shoulder-length grey hair beamed up at her. "Well, hello. And who must you be?"

Bella wondered if this woman was related to Dawn. Was it her grandmother? "Yes, hi. I'm looking for Dawn Heartfelt. She lived here with her parents."

The woman tilted her head and shrugged. "Nobody here by that name. Sorry, you must have the wrong house."

"No, I'm sure this is the house. She lived here about eleven years ago with her parents."

"Well, I don't know anyone by that name, but I have lived here for about seven years. The original house was burned down so they rebuilt. I never knew the previous owners. Sorry."

Bella's stomach flipped. *Burned down! The house was burned down.* "Do you know if anyone got hurt?"

"I can't tell you, Miss."

Bella nodded. "Okay, thank you." The woman smiled, closing the door. She walked to the car, feeling defeated.

She stopped by the local library and asked the librarian about archived newspapers from around news events in Williamstown nine to ten years ago. "It's all stored digitally, but here, I can show you over on the computers and how to do your search." The lady brought Bella over to the computer area and clicked on a number of buttons before showing Bella how to search for the digital information.

"Thanks. I think I've got it."

Bella sat at the desk and typed in the search on online news events of Williamstown from nine years ago. A number of events came up, but they weren't relevant. She couldn't find anything in the deaths section or burning houses. She searched for an earlier time period but still nothing. When she typed in 2011, she found a few headlines of interest. The lady obviously got the timing a bit off, but nonetheless, here it was. **"PARENTS DIE IN SUSPICIOUS FIRE. SURVIVED BY THEIR DAUGHTER, DAWN."**

Chapter Forty-Eight

DESIRES

A few days later, Bella was still reeling about her discovery of Dawn's burning house. The article had mentioned Dawn surviving the fire, but where was she? Why did the police think the fire was suspicious? It couldn't have been a deliberate fire, could it?

She peered through her window with an unsettled feeling, a sense that someone was watching her. Heading out the back of her house, she gently crept through her backyard and reached the side gate with its small peephole. Looking through it, she searched for something unusual but couldn't see anything. She was being paranoid. Nobody was watching her. She was safe, and Marco would surely visit as soon as he arrived back from Perth.

Walking back inside the house, she couldn't stop looking outside. An Australia Post van stopped by the kerb. A stocky man ambled to her front door carrying a small package. She hadn't ordered anything. A sick feeling penetrated her stomach as she answered the door.

The man smiled. "I just need you to sign here."

She traced the electronic pen across the machine and signed. "Thank you." She took the small package and closed the door, suddenly noticing Marco parking his car by the kerb. She watched the man walk back into his van and drive off then placed the package behind her lamp in the living room.

As she started walking outside to greet Marco, Bella's body tingled at the way his casual attire hugged his body tight, displaying his strong core. He had a strong, confident presence and was so poised. She yearned for those manly arms to hold her tightly, but their current conflicted situation with her case ruled it out.

When Marco stepped on to the footpath, he smiled at Bella. She wanted to run to him and wrap her hands around him. She'd missed him more than she cared to admit.

Marco continued to walk towards her, but it was like he was moving in slow motion. A white car came racing towards him on the footpath. Bella froze for a brief second. He turned with a gasp but couldn't move in time. The speed was unimaginable as the car veered straight towards him over the nature strip. Bella ran. She ran with all her strength and pulled him by the collar of his shirt. He fell over the picket fence. The car continued driving straight ahead, missing him by an inch. It disappeared into the distance.

Bella helped him up off the ground. Marco wiped the blades of grass from his shirt, his cheeks flushed and his eyes dark. "Oh my God, Marco. Are you all right?"

He nodded. "I'm fine, but that damn car's gone. Did you get the number plate?"

Bella shook her head and led him inside, a sudden overwhelming emotion settling inside her. It looked like Jackson driving, but it couldn't be. Would he try to hurt Marco? Was he jealous? "I think it was Jackson driving."

He punched a number into his phone and spoke to his partner. "Yes, I want you to find Jackson and bring him in. See if he's got a white sedan with him and bring that in too. Call me when you've got him." He sighed. "Get crime scene out here. If it was Jackson, he just assaulted a detective."

He followed her inside and they stood awkwardly in the living room. Marco stared into her eyes. "Thank you. You saved me. If you weren't there, I would be toast by now."

Bella felt herself blush. "You're welcome." She fought back tears but one of them fell in spite of it. Marco wiped it off her cheek with a tender hand.

"I was scared, Marco. Scared that you'd be hurt or worse. I don't know how much more of this I can take."

He leaned in towards her and held her tightly, his hand massaging the back of her head. The warmth of his hands made her feel safe. His hands trailed the small of her back and her body shook with electricity. "I am so sorry you had to go through that. I missed you."

He broke away from her, fixing his gaze on her and parting his lips. Inches from her face, he gently kissed her on yearning lips. Bella deepened the kiss, wanting him like she'd never wanted anyone before. Their tongues danced and their arms wrapped around each other tightly.

Marco pulled away and touched her face. "I can't do this. Conflict of interest."

Bella nodded. "I know. I don't want you getting in trouble." She took a calming breath. "Why are you here?"

Marco knit his brows. "Checking in, making sure you're okay."

She moved away from him and walked to the kitchen, shaking the desire out of her body. "I'll grab you a strong drink. You look a bit rattled. Are you okay?"

"I'm fine," he said, avoiding her eyes.

In her mind's eye, Bella imagined his arms entwined around her waist, his hands gently massaging her whole body as she leaned into his warmth, his solid body, and his manly arms. She didn't want to think about Marco being seriously injured or worse, killed. That would've created a huge void in her life, but she had to fight those thoughts and the desires away. Moving back to reality, she poured him a whisky, turned, and handed it to him. In one gulp and the drink was gone.

Chapter Forty-Nine

JOURNAL

The person unlocked the door to the apartment, hefting a vase of artificial flowers and throwing it to the floor. Shards fell around the kitchen floor. The person stepped over the pieces of glass, holes grazing into the boot's sole. Slamming the fridge, the person picked up a jug of water and drank straight from the jug, trickles of water running down the person's chin.

Breathing heavily and putting away the water, the person kicked at the door of the fridge, seething with rage. "How dare Jackson get in my way! I was so damn close to finishing off Marco for good, and he had to interfere, running a botched job without any planning, trying to run him over. How stupid can he be? Working in such an impulsive, disorganised way? Little Miss Princess had to ruin it too. I had other plans. Again, she tries to get closer to that damn detective. I could do damage to Marco, but I have to focus on Bella now. I can't afford to not think with my head. I might be furious, but I need a clear head to put my plan into motion. It won't be long now, bitch Bella. Not long now. Just you wait."

After Marco left, Bella remembered the package she'd received hidden behind the lamp. She unwrapped it and flinched at the sight of a journal, displaying Bridget's name on it. Who would send Bridget's journal to her address?

Bella opened the journal and was aghast at what she was reading. One segment read:

That bitch, Dawn keeps harping on her stupid friend, Bella. Who cares that her father threw Dawn out and that Bella didn't welcome her in the home? Who cares? I was glad to make her forget Bella. Good old, Dawn believed me when I mentioned how Bella left school to get away from her and make new friends. It was even freaky when Dawn liked Josh who ended up kissing Bella at the party. Even if Bella didn't know that Dawn liked him, I managed to convince Dawn that Bella didn't care she liked Josh.

Another entry read:

Oh, today was amazing. I cannot believe that Dawn is gay after seeing her kiss that other girl, whose name I forgot. It was priceless to see the look on her face when I took a picture, stole Bella's phone, and sent it from her phone to the entire Year 10 level. It was great to see the look on Dawn's face when she realised Bella had sent it, even though it was me. A good deed for today. My plan to break up their friendship is working, even if she's gone to a new school. Whatever Bella tells her won't sink into Dawn's measly brain.

Bella continued reading, her chest tight.

Today Dawn wrote this stupid poem about her girlfriend in English class, so I grabbed her writing book when she wasn't looking. I ripped it out of her book, then made copies of it and handed it out to all the Year 10 students. Oh, the poor, sad look on Dawn's face was priceless. She is putty in my hand, and I have complete control of her life. That'll teach her for answering back at me.

Bella looked up from the journal and shook her head. She'd forgotten about those other times Bridget got between them. She'd told Dawn how she couldn't trust Bridget and here was the proof. Then Bella left and Bridget continued to bully Dawn.

She wondered if Bridget was truly dead. She had come to life in this stupid journal.

If Bridget was alive, she'd be the one stalking her right now, making her life a living hell as she did back then. It would be something she'd do. As silly as it sounded to Bella, she started to think that

Bridget's ghost was taunting her. But she was truly dead, right?

Bella wondered who had sent her this journal. Was it the killer playing games with her, wanting to be found through this journal? In any case, she had to give this to Marco for possible fingerprints.

Chapter Fifty

WORK VISIT

Bella walked her client to the door. "I'll see you next week." She closed the door behind her and moved close to Mari, who was sniffling and wiping her nose and eyes with a tissue. Her eyes were red and bloodshot. Black circles under her eyes made her look fatigued and pale around the rest of her face. She had her head bowed down, dabbing her eyes again with the tissue.

Mari looked up and forced a smile. "Hey, Bella. Nice client you have there."

"She is great. Always open to trying out new things. How are you doing?"

She lay down the tissue and shifted in her chair. "I don't know. It's been hard breaking up with Oscar, but I'll get through it. Eventually." Tears slid down her cheeks. "I promised myself I wouldn't cry."

"Can I do anything? Make you a tea or get you water?"

She sniffed and played with her gold bracelet. "I'm fine, but..."

At that moment, Marco walked in, beaming at the sight of Bella. "Hey, Bella. How about..." He stopped when he spotted Mari behind the counter. "Hi, Mari. I didn't see you there with your head down. Are you okay?"

She shrugged. "I've sworn off men. They're more trouble than they're worth you know?"

"Oh." He turned to Bella with an awkward smile.

"Mari's having a hard time." She looked to Mari. "Can I tell him?" Mari nodded. "Her boyfriend broke up with her after being together for about a year. It's an adjustment."

"I'm sorry. He's a jerk, and I'm sure you'll find someone truly right for you."

"Thanks." Mari turned away and snatched up files, placing them in a cabinet. She slammed them in angrily and turned to Bella. "Sorry. I'll be fine."

"Can we talk?" Marco asked.

Bella nodded. "Of course." She led him to her office.

He closed the door behind him and rushed up inches from her, the strong scent of his musky aftershave making her tingle. "Listen, about the journal. We couldn't find any prints on it, but we'll see if we can get an idea of any suspects. I wouldn't think the killer sent you the journal unless they wanted to send you a message or a piece of the puzzle."

Bella took a breath. "It has to be someone who knows something, even if they're not involved in Bridget's murder."

"It's possible. Anyway, I also have questions about Jackson."

"You found him?"

"No, we're still looking. But I have more digging to do about Jackson's past, so we're looking further. This might give us leads into his whereabouts." Bella nodded. "Jackson doesn't strike me as a killer. A stalker, maybe, but this type of killer is organised, and trying to run me over was a disorganised activity. Although even serial killers can make bad decisions, but I don't get that feeling here."

She suddenly remembered the incident about Dawn's house. "I'm sorry, but I got distracted in the past few days with what's been going on. I forgot to tell you about my old friend, Dawn. I need you to check something out."

"What is it?" Marco fixed his gaze on her, drawing closer. Bella explained what she'd found out about Dawn's house fire. "I hope you were only trying to get in touch with an old friend and not investigating." Bella said nothing. Marco scoffed. "Do you think she might have something to do with the stalking?"

Bella shrugged when a light knock on the door broke their discussion.

Mari came inside still sniffling. "I'll see you guys. I'm going home."

"Will you be okay?"

She nodded. "I'm visiting a friend. She'll cheer me up, get me back on track."

Bella walked over and touched her shoulder. "Well, if you need anything, call me anytime. I'll see you tomorrow, but if you're not feeling well, take the day off."

Mari half-smiled. "Thanks. I'll see how I go." She glanced between her and Marco. The look on her face suggested she suspected something between them.

After Mari closed the door, Marco said, "I'll need to work late tonight, and I'll look into the fire. I'll just put this down to you looking up an old friend." He frowned. "Are you going home?"

Bella frowned. "I've got paperwork to do, but it can wait. I'm going home."

"Let me drive you but keep your door locked and don't open it for anyone."

"Yes, sir, but I've got my own car."

"I'll follow you then."

He held on to the small of her back as they walked out of her office, Bella's flesh tingling with heat at his touch. She wondered if things would change between them after this case was over.

Over by the counter, she noticed letters that needed stamps and had to be posted. "I'll have to stop by the post office as it'll close soon. You don't need to wait." She scooped up the envelopes and placed them in her bag. A business card fell off the counter. She picked it up off the floor and glanced at it. It was for a doctor's office she didn't recognize. "Must be Mari's." She placed the card back on the counter.

"I'll go with you and no arguments."

She shook her head. "Fine, but you need to stop mollycoddling me. I have my friends to lean on."

His eyes became stern. "I'm worried about you. Please take this seriously, Bella. We will catch this person, but maybe you should skip the country."

Bella chuckled, then turned on the alarm and locked the door. She put Marco out of her mind as she climbed into her car. She turned on the motor and watched in her rear-view mirror as Marco followed her to the post office. Unfortunately, the space in her mind with thoughts of Marco turned to thoughts of Jackson, wondering what more he was hiding. He was clearly unstable. He had tried to push professional boundaries and attacked her, then he was suddenly everywhere, claiming to be protecting her. The man had tried to run over Marco. At least she was mostly sure it had been Jackson driving that car.

Chapter Fifty-One

RESEARCH

Early Saturday morning, Bella and Mari sat opposite Jamie and Liz at a small cafe in Carlton. The smells of fresh coffee beans and sweet pastries permeated the air. Customers arrived sporadically as Bella explained what had happened to Marco. She still couldn't bring herself to tell them about their secret kiss, even though she wanted to. The more people who knew, the worse it would be for his job.

"My goodness, Bella. Jackson sounds somewhat crazy after harassing you and then offering you pepper spray. Two ironic actions. I am curious about his motive," Jamie said.

Liz squinted in the glaring sunlight coming in through an open window. "He has to be your stalker. It all fits. He wants you, can't have you, and then makes your life a living hell. Oh, and he's a serial killer on top of all that."

Bella said, "I don't know, Liz. I get the feeling that Jackson's not my stalker. I think there's more to his story, but I don't know what else I can do. Maybe I could talk to him again and hope he'll give me something. A clue even."

Mari drew a hand through her hair. "I think you need to stay away from him, Bella."

Jamie shook her head with pursed lips. "She's right. That is ludicrous. You cannot risk your life by talking to Jackson. He may very well be your stalker. Stay away from him. Besides, isn't he still missing?"

Bella nodded, realising how stupid it was to get further involved. But she had to do something. Nothing much was happening on the police front, and she hoped to speed things up a bit. "You're right. I know. I'll stay away. I have to think of some other way to find out." She ventured into telling them about Dawn's house burning down.

Liz warmed her hands around the coffee mug. "Do you think your past with Dawn is related to what's happening now?"

Bella sat back against the chair. "I don't know what to believe anymore."

Jamie tapped her fingers across her other hand, in deep thought. She picked up her cafe latte and took a sip while Bella blew on her hot chocolate. "If only we could get Jackson's authorisation to access his medical records. If he had next of kin who could act on his behalf, then we could access his records that way. I mean, he might have a mental health history."

Liz smiled to herself, appearing to be in her own world. "Girls, I've got it. I know a friend of a friend who can access Jackson's medical records. Easy peasy."

Jamie's face turned pale as she drew back. Clasping her hands, she said, "Are you insane? Do you have any awareness of how many privacy acts exist simply to protect confidentiality?"

Liz shrugged. "I know, but this person who shall remain nameless has done it before. She only does it in the most dire of circumstances. She's untraceable and can get in there easily and quickly. I say we do it."

Jamie turned away. "Absolutely not."

"Don't even go there," said Mari. "If Jackson finds out, who knows what he'll do."

"I agree with Mari and Jamie. This is too risky," said Bella. "Leave it alone."

Liz sighed. "You guys are too anxious for your own good. Take a risk sometime in your life." She tilted her head then finished the last remnants of her espresso. Wiping her mouth with a serviette, Liz looked at Bella. "Even you said the police were not getting anywhere. That detective Marco won't tell you anything as a civilian, so I say we do our own sleuthing. Believe me, she's very good and she won't be traced."

Jamie scoffed. "No, Liz. I forbid it."

Bella's head told her no, but her heart felt it was the right thing to do when lives were at stake. But she was also afraid of the risk. "I don't know, Liz. Like I said, it's too risky."

Liz nodded. "Listen, think about it. Sleep on it and get back to me tomorrow."

Jamie turned to Bella. "Do not even think about this. Put it completely out of your mind."

Bella fixed her gaze on Jamie. "Marco and the police are digging into Jackson's past. They have the resources we don't. Please leave it alone. Give the police time to do their job, and let's leave it at that. Okay, Liz? You getting involved endangers you."

"Think of dear Martha, Liz. You were threatened before, remember?" Jamie teared up and wiped her nose.

Liz turned to Bella. "Fine, ladies. I'll leave it for now." She took a breath. "Now, what's going on between you and the detective? You're always blushing when you talk about him, and you use his first name. Is something going on between you two?" Bella's heart raced and she stared at her hands. She didn't want to say anything in fear that things would turn out badly for him. "Earth to Bella."

She broke out of her thoughts. "We might've got a bit close, but we're not going to do anything more while this case is going. His job is on the line."

Liz leaned forward, rubbing her hands. "Oh my God! When you say 'anything more' do you mean that something's already happened? I want to hear all the sexy details."

Jamie chuckled. "You have no maturity, Liz. Besides, this is a risky situation and could cost the detective his job. Disciplinary action, even."

Bella pressed her lips together. "I can't give you any details, but we might've shared a kiss. I don't want to get him into trouble, Liz, so please don't say anything to anyone."

"You are one nasty girl, Bella. But I must say, he is hot and spicy." Mari chuckled.

Liz's eyes dilated. "Oh, so what was it like?" Bella was silent. "You can trust that I won't say anything, girl." She sighed. "Come on, it's easy. Just say yes it was a great kiss or no it was like kissing your brother."

Bella peered past Liz, her hands shaking.

Your brother...brother...

Chapter Fifty-Two

FRIENDSHIP

Frozen in her seat at the cafe, Bella's mind reeled with images of her brother lying still on the ground. Her mind flashed back briefly to the day her mother got drunk when she was eleven and her brother was two. All those years, her mind trailed back to her dear brother.

Her father was at work, and she'd walked into her house after school, her mother drunk and lying on the couch. She had passed out again. Where was Davie? She searched his bedroom but he wasn't anywhere to be seen. She walked out of his room and into the playroom but couldn't see him. His shoe was propped near the beanbag. Was he playing hide and seek?

As she got closer and veered towards the window, the cord from the curtain had been lifted. She froze at the sight. Davie was stock-still and deathly-white with the curtain's cord wound around his neck. She rushed over to his body and shook him.

"Wake up, Davie. Davie wake up."

Tears formed in her eyes, and she screamed. Her mother rushed into the room, and with one look at Davie's dead body, fell back and fainted. Her father came into the house after Bella called him at work. He waltzed into the house sometime later and for the first time in her miserable life, he actually showed emotion. He then beat her mother to a pulp, almost killing her. If Bella hadn't stopped him, her mother would also be in a body bag. Her father had paid a doctor for a home visit to tend to her mother's wounds. Her mother had never reported him for abuse, possibly due to her own guilt.

❦❦❦❦❦❦ ❦❦❦❦❦

Bella put a gentle hand on her chest. She felt Liz's hand squeezing her own, a pained look on her friend's face.

"I'm so sorry, Bella. I didn't think how stupid that was until after I said it. I'm really sorry." Liz drew a hand through her hair.

Bella gave her a reassuring smile. "It's okay. I can't keep tip-toeing around the word 'brother'. It will always hurt, but I'm not going to ban you girls from saying whatever's on your mind. It's all good."

"I know it's probably none of my business, but are you okay?" Mari asked.

Bella didn't want to dredge that up when Mari was grieving over her relationship. "I'll share that another time, Mari if you don't mind."

Her eyes softened. "Not at all, Bella. I'm here for you."

Liz fidgeted. "Tell us about you, Mari."

Mari's blue eyes dimmed, and she rubbed her hands down her pants. Her petiteness was endearing. "Let's see. I love doing web design for clients, but some of them can be particularly demanding. They ask for changes and when I make them, they ask to return to the original design. All that time wasted."

"I assume you charge them for that extra time?" said Jamie.

Mari turned to Jamie and scraped a hand through her copper highlights. "I don't charge them. I feel bad because I love helping people, and if I start charging extra, they'll hate me for it. I might not even get repeat business."

Liz tilted her head. "But it's business. If you put in the time, they should pay you. That time could've been spent on other clients."

Mari nodded. "I know you're technically right, but I feel bad about it. A friend of mine tells me, 'Mari you're too nice for your own good.' Maybe she's right, and I'm working on thinking more about me."

Sitting beside them was a young girl of about five and a woman assumed to be her mother, sharing a meal of chips. A cup of coffee rested near the plate and the girl reached out for it, tilting it. Drops of liquid fell on the tablecloth. When her mother pulled her hand away, she slapped the girl hard. The little girl cried when the mother said, "Silly girl. You've made a mess."

Mari rose from her seat and put her arms around the little girl. "It's okay. It was an accident. Not to worry." She stroked the girl's hair with a look of endearment, but the woman pursed her lips.

The woman rose from her seat, hands across her hips. "Leave now! This is none of your business."

Mari ignored the woman, returning to her seat with a despondent expression. Bella was surprised at the way Mari stood up for the little girl. She had never seen anyone filled with so much love for a child.

Bella reached for Mari who drew into herself, appearing miles away. "Are you okay?"

Mari nodded, looking as though she was fighting back tears. "I hate seeing mothers hit their children. It's barbaric. Why have children if you can't care for them properly?" She cleared her throat. "I'm sorry." She looked up at Bella and her friends.

Jamie said, "You've got a big heart. I love kids too, and there is a prevalence of abuse out there."

Liz nodded, whispering, "I feel you, Mari."

A few minutes passed by and the tension around eased. Having forgotten about the incident with the girl, Liz spoke up. "Anyway, Marco is gorgeous though, and so manly that I'd have him myself if he wasn't into you."

"Oh, Bella. Forgive Liz's crude remarks. She can't help herself." Her eyes darkened as Jamie faced her friend. "Be very careful. The timing is the worst, but it is a great thing that you haven't gone beyond a kiss. At least for now."

"For now," Liz reiterated. She rubbed her hands, beaming.

Bella avoided Jamie's eyes. "I know, Jamie. It's the right thing to do."

Bella was thankful to have both her friends in her life and was worried about Marco's profession being impacted because of lust. Or was there more to it? It was crazy to even think about romance when this killer was lurking around. The sooner this was over, the better.

Bella looked at Liz. If Liz's friend was as great as she said she was, it couldn't do any harm to get this woman access to those records. Bella scolded herself. It was so unethical. She put it out of her mind.

Chapter Fifty-Three

SAVED BY THE BELL

The following Saturday night, Marco slipped into bed, imagining Bella beside him. He pictured her eyes that spoke volumes, the innocence, yet the strength in them. He pictured his hand buried in her silky smooth hair and holding her in his arms. He wanted to put a smile on her face and take away that sombre, far-away look she'd had a few times. He wanted her pain to disappear, but in the meantime, he savoured their special kiss.

As he was falling into a light slumber, the phone jolted him fully awake. He lifted himself up from bed and reached out for the phone on his bedside table.

He answered the phone, a sick feeling in his stomach. *Please let Bella be okay.* "Tim. What's wrong?"

"Claudia was stabbed tonight."

He sat up, rubbing his eyes. "Oh, shit. What happened?"

"An intruder broke into her home, but luckily, the perp left before doing further damage. She's in hospital, but with minor wounds."

"Which hospital? I'll meet you there."

"Royal Melbourne."

Marco hung up and made it out the door in twenty minutes.

Once he reached the hospital ward, he shuddered at the bruises around Claudia's eyes and the bandage across her upper right chest. Tim was standing near the window, pulling towards the blinds until he turned.

"Hi Claudia. How are you feeling?"

She chuckled. "Like I've been stabbed."

He ignored her humour. "Tell me what happened."

She shifted herself upright. "I was in the middle of making dinner when I heard a noise from the back door. I didn't turn on the light, and when I got there, this person jumped me. They held a knife and I tried to fight them, but they stabbed me in my upper chest. They lifted the knife up again, and I thought for sure I'd be dead this time. I was expecting a friend for dinner and the doorbell rang. The intruder got distracted by the sound, and in that instant, I ran for my life to the door, expecting the person to jump me again. They left."

"Did you get a good look at the person?"

"A bulky figure, and very strong, wearing a hooded jacket, gloves, and baggy jeans."

Tim stood closer to her bedside. "Any idea if it was a man or woman?"

Claudia shrugged. "It was dark, and I couldn't tell. I assumed it was a man because of their strength and bulky build. Sorry I can't give you more than that."

"No worries, Claudia. When you're up to it, we'll need you to give a formal statement in writing at the station." Marco handed her his business card.

She angled her head. "Wait. I remember now. The person said something when they stabbed me." She shifted her weight in the bed and winced as if in pain. "They said 'you've been marked.' Also, the way this person moved was familiar. Like I've seen them before."

Marco winced and stared at Tim who stood wide-eyed. "Give it time. I'm sure it'll come back to you." He wasn't surprised by the connection.

Marco and Tim walked out of the ward towards the parking area.

"What do you think?" Marco asked.

"I think the perp got spooked by the friend so left."

"Hmm, and they're making mistakes. The MO has changed, and I'm assuming maybe Claudia might know something. Something the perp wants silenced," said Marco.

Tim nodded. "Let's head to the station and get more on Jackson. I have a hunch he may not be the killer, but he knows something."

Chapter Fifty-Four

AT HER OWN PERIL

B ella sighed with relief at the end of her workday, having treated five clients with similar problems. She relished home for the pure joy of soaking into an invigorating bath, to focus only on lowering her high adrenaline levels.

She walked her last client to the door then closed it behind her. Mari sat deep in thought behind the receptionist desk. She was chewing on her nails, her eyes peering into the distance. Probably thinking about her possessive boyfriend again or the cafe incident. She appeared to be struggling over the break-up, big-time. She was about to offer a soothing comment, but then Mari put her head down and pressed stamps onto envelopes for appointment letters. *Why bother her? She'll be fine.*

Bella decided to approach her briefly. "Mari, I wanted to say again how great you were with that girl. The mother shouldn't have slapped her hand."

Mari's eyes hardened. "It kills me how mothers treat their children like that. I love kids, and one day I hope to have them, but that little girl didn't deserve that." Her shoulders drooped and she stared into her hands.

"Well you did a good thing." Bella ambled back into her office and grasped her bag. She rummaged inside to find her car key when something slipped out of the bag. It was a butterfly charm. *This isn't my charm. Whose charm is it and how did it get in my bag?* She picked it up, turning it over. *Dawn liked butterflies.* A chill ran over her back. Had Dawn broken into her house? She might've slipped the charm in there as a way of making a statement. Did Dawn want her to realise she was her stalker? No, she couldn't be? Or was it Jackson? He might've known that Dawn liked butterflies.

Her mobile phone buzzed in her bag. Looking at the screen, Marco's number came up. Was he checking in or had something happened?

Whatever it was, she had to respond to her phone.

Mari came into her office. "I wanted to know if you had any mail for me to post. I'm heading out to the post office soon."

Bella found a few reports that needed to be sent to old clients. "Sure. On my desk, but can you give me a few minutes? I have to take this." She pointed to the phone.

Mari beamed. "Oh, of course. I'll come back."

She partially closed the door behind her when Bella answered her phone.

"Hey, Marco. How are you?"

"Bella, listen..." His voice cut out from interference in the call or a poor connection.

"Sorry, what did you say?"

"Claudia was attacked."

Her world spun around her in that moment, and she wondered if she heard him correctly. "I'm sorry, what did you say?"

"Claudia was stabbed late last night when an intruder broke into her home. Luckily, she got away. She made it to the police station, and she's now in hospital. She remembered something the attacker said this morning."

Bella's vision blurred as she gripped her phone, sweating profusely over her forehead. She remembered to breathe. "Please don't tell me."

"Sorry, but the intruder said to her, 'You've been marked.' This can't be a coincidence."

"I'll be right there."

"I'm coming by to bring you to the station. We'll keep you safe."

"No need. I've got my own car. You don't need to come here. I'll leave now and meet you at the station."

"I'm getting closer and, right now, I'm searching databases and have a few calls to make. What I've discovered so far is that Dawn has fallen off the grid, but I know she was disfigured from the fire. Her parents died but she got out in time, and her face was damaged, so I'm assuming..."

"Plastic surgery?" said Bella.

"Most likely, but I'm closing in and backtracking from that fire incident. I'll keep you informed. I'm coming to you so wait for me. I won't be long."

Bella sighed, resigning herself to the situation. "Fine. I'll wait then."

She hung up, her mind casting her back to the butterfly charm in her bag. It must've fallen into her bag from the reception counter by accident when she had picked up those envelopes. Was it Mari's butterfly charm? Reception was Mari's domain.

Turning off her computer and retrieving her bag and the letters, Bella rushed out of her office. She wasn't waiting for Marco.

Spotting Mari over by the front desk, she said, "Here you go." Bella handed her the letters and forced a smile. "I really have to get going. I'll see you tomorrow then. If you wouldn't mind closing up." Her heart beat a mile a minute as she scrambled out towards the door.

Mari approached her. "What's wrong? You look frazzled."

"Ah, nothing. I have an appointment with the ah...dentist. I'll be late otherwise."

Mari moved even closer within inches of her face. "You know, I can always tell when you lie. I can tell you're lying now."

I can always tell when you lie... She had heard that before. Bella froze, her throat dry. "I'm not lying. I have to go." She turned around and made her way towards the door. Footsteps sounded behind her. Her spine tingled but she kept up her pace, finally reaching the door. She felt a prick in her shoulder.

"Oh no you don't. You're mine now, bitch."

Bella felt woozy and struggled to stand. She fell back, and the last thing she heard was, "I heard your conversation with Marco. I'm not stupid. And he'll never find us."

"Dawn..." Bella said. Before she could finish, the world went black.

Chapter Fifty-Five

A PAST MEMORY

Marco sat in front of his computer at the police station with Tim sitting beside him.

"Jackson was admitted into a psychiatric facility about eleven years ago when he was nineteen years of age. Diagnosed with borderline personality traits. But, get this. He had a girlfriend who was diagnosed with narcissistic personality disorder, not long after her parents died in a house fire. Now, there's no sign of this girlfriend. After the treatment, she disappeared."

Marco froze on the spot and moved his hand away from the mouse. His eye twitched. That newspaper article about the house fire came into the forefront of his mind. His heart raced. *Could the woman be Dawn?* "My God! That article I told you about, Tim. The one that Bella found out about. The house fire. Do you think...?"

"It's possible," said Tim, answering his unspoken question.

"We need to focus on Bella's friend, Dawn." He tapped his fingers on the desk, staring out at the few detectives who were busily talking and interviewing witnesses for other cases. Others, including police officers were out on the field. He loved the buzz of the office. It got his adrenaline spiking after solving puzzles. "So, let's talk through what we know so far." He cleared his throat. "We know that Bridget and Margaret had a tranquiliser in their system, so the perp could easily transport them to the kill location. We know that both of them were posed in a way to show degradation and humiliation, as if to say, 'these women are rubbish', given they were both dumped at a household waste site. We have two people with serious mental health issues, and possibly susceptible to anger and interpersonal issues, right?"

"And we're thinking revenge?" Tim said.

"But if it is Dawn, why target Bella now, assuming they were true friends?" He bowed his head. "What does Claudia have to do with all this?"

Tim shifted. "Jackson, and assuming it's Dawn who was his girlfriend, may have lived together. If we chase the money trail, then there might be something."

Marco keyed in details, searching last known addresses for Jackson. He had lived in Perth for a while, but then moved to Melbourne more recently, and before Bridget's murder. That couldn't be a coincidence.

"Hang on. There's a place he owned in a remote area of Geelong."

Tim leaned in, staring at the screen. "It hasn't been sold, though. He might be renting it out, or he stays there from time to time."

He picked up his desk phone and called John, the forensics expert. "Listen, can you dig into Dawn Heartfelt. You'll have better luck than me in finding her. I want to know everything you can get about her. Previous addresses, purchases, friends, family, medical details, the lot. I need this yesterday."

"Sure thing. I'll get onto it now," said John.

Marco ended the call up when his mobile phone buzzed on his desk. He checked the screen, displaying an unknown number. "Hello, Marco speaking."

"Marco, it's Claudia. I know who attacked me."

Chapter Fifty-Six

A DEATH TRAP

Bella's head seemed to weigh a ton. Her shoulders ached. She slowly opened her eyes and tried to roll over, but her arm was caught. She blinked away the blurriness. There was a length of rope tied around her wrist. She looked down at her feet. They were in stirrups. She was strapped to a bed. Gasping, she looked around a room with bare walls, a sterile stench, dusty linoleum flooring, and a silver tray of implements on a mobile table. She looked closer at the implements and a chill ran down her spine. In the tray lay a scalpel, hammer, serrated knife, and scissors.

Mari, or Dawn; she corrected herself, was going to torture and then kill her like she had the others. The ropes cut deeply into her skin. She pulled, but the restraints wouldn't budge. As for the stirrups, she'd never untangle herself out of there.

Bella refused to give up without a fight. She wouldn't let the immobilising terror of this place deter her from getting out of here alive.

She could talk her way out of it. Could she stall for time? It was possible that Marco might find her, but she couldn't rely on that. Then the panic began to set in. She was going to die here. She was going to die at twenty-seven and alone without ever having lived. She realised she had spent her entire life hiding and it had cost her. If she ever got out of here, she'd change that. Bella had value and deserved to live, and she would no longer let her past define her.

Her eyes turned to the noise of footsteps in the distance. She clenched her teeth when Mari strolled into the room, glaring at Bella.

"Well, well, I see you're adapting to my place. Any last words?"

Bella's body shook and her teeth clattered as if she was freezing. She fought back her fear to work on her emotional state to save herself. "Why are you doing this, Mari? Or should I say, Dawn?"

"I knew you'd figured it out after that stupid detective's call."

"You didn't answer my question."

She gloated and hovered over Bella. "Hmm. Let's see. It was the time you teamed up with Bridget to bully and hurt me, the time you tarnished my name around the school, and the time you couldn't give a rat's ass about me when I visited you at home.

Just leaving me alone to fend off that bitch, Bridget. You only cared about yourself and didn't care that Bridget taunted me day in, day out. You used me for your own damn control, bitch. You never cared."

Bella shook her head. "No, that was all Bridget and my dad. She set me up because she was jealous of our friendship. She was trying to break us up. I never did any of that. She bullied me too. My dad lied. I didn't say those things. I still wanted to be friends."

Dawn chuckled. "You'd say anything to get out of this, but it's not that easy. If you could rewind and change the past, that would be the only damn thing that'd save you."

Bella had to win this argument. "But you know the type of person I am. You were my receptionist and a very good one. We had a great working relationship, and I thought we were friends. You, me, Jamie, and Liz."

"It was all an act on my part. I hated all of you the entire time." She scoffed. "I even read your silly book about moving beyond grief, and how you have to go through all these steps to process your grief. What a bunch of hogwash. Grief is grief, and nothing will ever make me forget and move beyond what you and Bridget did to me. You made me lose everything. You abandoned me."

"No, Dawn, please listen to me. I was bullied by Bridget too, and she set you up all those times. I'm innocent of all that. You have to believe me. We were close once. I loved you like a sister and would never hurt you."

"The only thing I believe is that you're a power-hungry bitch. Pretending to like people and then discarding them like rubbish. You went after that guy I liked too."

Bella tilted her head. "What guy?"

"Josh. I saw you kissing him."

Bella knit her brows. "I didn't even know you liked him, and we only went out a few times. If I knew you cared about him, I wouldn't have gone out with the guy."

"Likely story."

"I really didn't know you liked him, Dawn." She became short of breath. "I'm sorry."

"You'll say anything just to manipulate me."

Bella couldn't win a war against a narcissist. She had obviously not known the real Dawn ever. She had kept her true colours to herself until she could no longer hide it because of her experiences. "Why did you kill Martha?"

She threw her head back. "I was in love with George, her husband, and she got between us. The bastard went back to her, and I was alone yet again. I'm always alone."

Her teeth rattled. "Oh no! You're the woman he was having an affair with. That was the time you were upset over Oscar. Was Oscar really George?"

"Yes, Oscar was a made-up name, and Martha had to pay. Even after she died, I tried to get back with him, but he refused. He didn't want to see me. That hurt even more because she was out of our lives, and he could never go back to her when she was dead."

"But he was her husband, not yours."

Dawn shrugged. "He's lucky I didn't kill him, but like I said, even after Martha died, he didn't want me back."

"He was grieving," Bella said. She had to get answers and stall for time. "What happened to you over the years, Dawn? Please help me understand you."

She chuckled. "For your next book, bitch?"

"I need to know what happened to you." She needed to get Dawn talking, but was she too smart for that?

Chapter Fifty-Seven

STILL IN DANGER

Dawn planted her hands across her hips, peering into the distance. "Jackson saved me. He was my lover and helped me burn the house down. My parents deserved it. They paid for men to have sex with me, and they put photos of me online." She glared at Bella and clenched her teeth. "I saw my parents getting aroused when a man tortured me or had sex with me from the age of fifteen. Not only was that bitch Bridget bullying me, but my parents got rich from my pain. In the end, I adapted like I always do, and I got my vengeance and killed them. They damn well deserved it, just like the others."

Chills ran down Bella's spine. Oh, the terror of her story. "I am so sorry, Dawn. I wish I'd been there for you. I wish you'd told me this when we were at school. I could've got you help."

"Nobody helps, Bella. Don't be so damn naive. Stop pretending you care."

Bella had to get through to her. "I understand what you were going through because my bastard father was abusive towards me too. My mother was always drunk. You didn't deserve any of that, and they should've been locked up. I'm sorry."

Bella noticed her eyes softening, tears starting to form. It lasted a brief moment, but then her eyes grew cold again.

"Don't try your damn psychology on me. It won't work."

"I'm not doing that. I know what it's like to be treated like shit and to feel rejected and unloved. No-one should feel that way. I cared about you, Dawn. You were my closest friend. You have to believe that."

Dawn ignored her. She glanced at the silver tray and picked up a scalpel, turning it over in her hand. She gripped it and headed close to Bella who turned her eyes away.

Stalling for more time, she said, "Dawn, I saw your butterfly charm. I guess you still like them after all these years."

She squeezed the scalpel into her hand, blood trickling down. "I couldn't be Dawn anymore. She was a loser, and weak, letting that bitch Bridget bully her for years. I needed a new face, a new identity, and now I have the power to rid the world of all these evil bitches. If you ask me, I'm doing the world a favour."

Bella had to appeal to some sense of her humanity, if she had one. "The fire. Is that why you had the surgery?"

Mari chuckled. "My parents deserved it, and I only got disfigured because I got so aroused watching them burn. Hell, it was worth my face burning just to see them get exactly what they deserved. I'd do it all over again. I enjoyed killing Bridget, too."

"I understand. I would've killed Bridget myself if I had the power, but let's talk this through." Her voice had obviously changed from the fire inhalation.

Dawn chuckled. "Still trying to get your way. You couldn't kill. You're not strong enough."

Stall for time! Make this about her. "I saw that doctor's card on your desk. Did you see him recently after all these years?"

She scrutinised her. "I was getting facial pain, probably from all the stress you've given me. I just checked in, but pity you saw the card. Not that it mattered anyway, because I got you in the end."

"Please, Dawn. I loved you. I still love you." She edged close to Bella, her eyes glistening as she held out the scalpel. "No, please don't. No!"

Dawn gagged her with a dirty cloth. She angled the scalpel and cut deeply into her chest, the blood trickling. Bella yelled through her gag as pain exploded across her chest. She was going to die. With the second cut below the first one, she gasped at the pain, possibly worse than death. The next cut went even deeper as Dawn twisted it slowly into her flesh.

Bella cried and closed her eyes, trying desperately to imagine a safe place. She couldn't breathe, and the sickly smell of tangy blood blurred her vision. The room was spinning, and Dawn's face became monstrous and ghastly as she flicked her tongue over her lips, smiling to herself. Dawn lay the scalpel aside and buried her face into Bella's chest to lick off the blood. Her fingers prodded and pressed hard into one of her wounds when Bella passed out.

Chapter Fifty-Eight

TICKING CLOCK

Marco ignored all the speed limits as he raced to Bella's workplace. If anything happened to Bella, he'd never forgive himself. She was everything to him, and he should've protected her more than he had. He shouldn't have let her out of his sight. Too late now. He had to get to her before anything happened.

He rushed out of his car and banged on Bella's door at her workplace. He huffed, noticing the blinds were drawn. No response. He banged again, but nothing. *Oh, Christ*! He had to get to that location.

Stepping back into his car and driving off, his phone rang. He responded on his Bluetooth. "Tim, sorry. I couldn't wait. I told John to call for back-up, but I had to rush here." He was short of breath. "Listen, Bella wasn't at work. She's either on her way to the station or she's been kidnapped. Either way I'm off to that location."

"Wait for back up, Marco. Don't do this on your own."

"No time to wait. They can meet me there."

"Fine. I'll meet you at the location," Tim said.

He sped all the way to Geelong, cursing and swearing at slow drivers. He put on his siren so drivers would let him through. He had to get there in time. His hands slipped on the steering wheel and his shoulders remained tightly clenched. His body shivered and he ignored his parched throat.

He was fifteen minutes away from Jackson and Dawn's place, and he was sure that Jackson was possibly hiding there now. *The bastard!* The trouble he put Bella through. Oh, no! This was taking too long. What if Bella didn't have fifteen minutes?

His heart almost exploded, and he couldn't breathe properly.

Hang on, Bella. I'm coming!

Chapter Fifty-Nine

FRAGILE STATE

Bella woke up to find herself a bloody mess, the caked up dried blood making her feel nauseous. She struggled to breathe through the sharp pain throbbing in her chest. Dehydrated, she wondered how long it had been since she had been cut.

Muffled voices in the distance caught her attention. She wondered if the deeper voice belonged to Jackson. No doubt they were working as a team with all these murders.

She heard the creak of a floorboard. They were coming for her. Panic rose and doubled when Jackson ran towards her. "Oh, Bella. I'm so sorry. I'm here now. You'll be fine." He touched her face and leaned in, kissing her softly on the lips. Bella turned, but he forced his lips on hers. Suddenly, Dawn pulled him away from her.

Dawn shoved him. "Get off her. She doesn't deserve your pity, Jackson. Besides, last time I checked you and I are still fucking whenever we feel like it. Not that I give a crap who you kiss or fondle."

Jackson poked her in the chest. "You can't do this. I've put up with those other women, but not Bella. She's special, and kind, and doesn't deserve this."

Dawn pressed her lips hard together. "I'm sorry, Jackson, but this one's mine. Go find yourself another toy to play with. She's a bully and a bitch and doesn't care about you. She loves Marco."

Jackson turned towards Bella. "You can learn to love me, right?"

Stay alive. Bella lied. "Of course I can. I care about you, Jackson. Marco and I are not involved." Bella tried not to let the disgust seep into her face when she had a sudden thought. "You sent me Bridget's journal, didn't you, Jackson?"

"I wanted to help." He grinned and stroked her face. "Oh, Bella. I knew you'd realise. I didn't want to run Marco over the way I almost did, but he was between us. You didn't give us a chance, but now we can have that chance." He kissed her again, his tongue penetrating her mouth, and Bella had to stop herself from gagging. She kissed him back, imagining he was Marco. Jackson was her only salvation. Could he convince Dawn to let her go? She had to play along with Jackson for now.

His hands roamed over her open shirt as he gently dabbed on her wounds with a wet cloth. He trailed his fingers down to her belly button then almost touched her further down before

Dawn got behind him. "Oh, that's enough. She's mine now. Please go."

Jackson shook his head. "No, you're not hurting her. I'll call the police this time."

Bella noticed that Dawn held something behind her back. When she looked at the silver tray, the hammer had disappeared. Before she could warn Jackson, Dawn lifted up her right arm and struck Jackson over the back of his head. He toppled backwards, his eyes rolling while Dawn broke his fall. She lay him on the floor, then shoved him in a corner of the room and tied up his hands with a thick rope. She walked back to Bella with a smirk. "I guess he can't save you now. No-one can."

Her mouth went dry, terror no doubt showing in her eyes. "Please, Dawn. Let's talk about this. I know how hard your life's been and it's unfair that you had to suffer. No-one should be bullied. Bridget got exactly what she deserved and so did her friend. I hated both of them. They were bitches and deserved to die. Please let me go."

Dawn's features again softened, her eyes glazing over as she stared, lost in thought. She returned to the present and stuffed the cloth back in Bella's mouth. "You will shut up now. I've had enough of your crap. Bitches like you leave misery in your wake. Abandon people like rubbish. I'm doing the world a favour by discarding rubbish." She turned back to her tray and clutched the serrated knife.

Bella couldn't breathe as she stared hard at the knife. She shook her head, forcing her body to move but it wouldn't budge. She was trapped in her restraints.

Bella shuddered from the pain. Dawn held up the knife, admiring it in the dim light. She swung it up high and stabbed Bella in the lower abdomen. She groaned in pure agony, her body shifting on the bed. The pain was unbearable, and she felt her breathing grow shallow, her energy draining out of her. Dawn lifted the knife up again and stabbed her on the other side of the abdomen. Again, Bella drew back and closed her eyes, imagining another time and place to try and escape this hell. If she could only numb the pain, she could manage it. The wounds weren't too deep, but she would eventually bleed out.

Dawn's eyes lit up. She reached out and touched the blood. She brought her bloodied finger up to her mouth and licked it. She was aroused by the blood. Bella vomited then gasped for breath as the pain in her abdomen knocked the wind out of her.

"Oh, you fucking bitch. I didn't tell you to vomit all over the fucking bed." She slapped her hard across the cheek, but she felt nothing. She numbed herself to the pain and took calming breaths. *I can deal with the pain. I can deal with the pain.* She had to.

Dawn scurried out of the room and came back in with a bucket and sponge. She wiped it off the bed and off Bella, allowing it to drip into the bucket as she held it at the edge of the bed. She left the room again, and Bella closed her eyes to shut out the pain, clenching her teeth so hard she thought they might break.

Dawn returned with a smile. "I guess I'll take my time with you. I plan to savour you. How about we use the hammer to break the bones in your hands first? Then we'll move to other parts. But don't worry just yet. We've got all night. I'll give you a bit of a break. Don't miss me too much." Beside the bed, she grabbed a bandage and pressed it onto the wound, making Bella scream, then taped it tight. Obviously, she wanted Bella to heal in order to create new wounds. Prolong the suffering.

Dawn left her side then dragged Jackson out of the room. She closed the door. Bella could almost breathe again. The thought of her bones breaking was too much to bear, so she pulled at the restraints again with all her strength, but nothing budged. She was doomed.

Chapter Sixty

HER SAVING GRACE

Bella's eyes flicked open and closed as the pain and fear stopped her from sleeping. She had to stay awake and find a way to get out of this dungeon. It had been a long time since seeing Dawn, and she figured at least an hour had gone by. She might've gone out. The longer she stayed away, the better the chance of the authorities finding her, either dead or alive.

The coppery sharp smell of blood and her vomit filled the room. She needed to empty her bladder and feared she might have to do it right there on the bed.

The room was dark with no windows, and it appeared to be a basement of some kind. Bella realised that this was obviously Dawn's kill room when she noticed bits of clothing stuck in piles over in a corner. Streaks of blood covered parts of the walls.

Footsteps sounded in the distance. *Oh, no*, she was coming back. Bella's clammy skin resumed its copious sweating, and she gasped as she clenched her jaw and tried to stop hyperventilating. Shaking her head, she started seeing black spots around her, not able to accept her impending demise. Her body became weak and weighted, and the pain in her back was gruelling. What did she do to deserve this? Dawn was going to break her bones. How could she numb herself to that kind of pain?

The footsteps got closer. She closed her eyes to avoid the evil in Dawn's eyes. The footsteps didn't sound right. They didn't sound like Dawn's. They were heavier. Bella opened her eyes and let out a sob.

"Oh, my God! Bella." Marco got her out of the stirrups, wincing when he saw her wounds. Bella wiggled her legs to return sensation to them. Pins and needles ran through her, setting off the pain in her abdomen again. She groaned. He reached for the knotted rope around her wrists, untying it from the steel bar forming the head of the bed. He struggled with the knot. "Are you okay?"

Bella ignored his question. "Hurry, I don't know where she is."

Marco nodded. "Sorry, I'll be quick. But I've got back-up on the way. I couldn't wait for them. I had to get to you, Bella. They should be here soon." His eyes softened. "It's going to be all right. I didn't see Dawn anywhere. She must've gone out."

After untying one of the ropes, Marco worked on the other one. Bella tried to sit up, but the pain made her weak. She had to push through the pain now and worry about her injuries later. They still weren't safe.

"This knot's even worse. Where the hell did she learn how to do this?"

Marco suddenly went limp and fell back against the ground. Dawn was holding the hammer, and blood gushed out of the side of Marco's head. "No!" Bella screamed. *No.* She sobbed. He couldn't be dead.

Dawn stared at Bella and shook her head. "How the hell did that bastard find me?"

As she stared at Marco, wondering what to do with him, Bella swung out her right leg, aiming it towards Dawn. She kicked her hard in the face as she jerked backwards and fell back, hitting her head against the ground. As soon as she fell, Dawn lifted herself back up with a twisted expression on her face. She glared at Bella and charged. Punching her hard in the eye, Bella almost blacked out, but she refused to let Dawn kill her. She had to fight to stay awake or she'd be dead. This time, she wouldn't prolong her death. She'd make it quick.

Bella desperately pulled at the rope but it wouldn't budge. She watched in horror as Dawn grabbed the serrated knife aiming it towards her eye. Bella's chest pumped, but she fought hard against the terror and got clear in her mind. Bella leaned back, trying to dodge the knife as Dawn slashed it in the air, narrowly missing her eye. Bella lifted up her knee and kicked her square in the face. Dawn dropped the knife on the bed and fell back on top of Marco who groaned. Bella grabbed the knife with her right hand and cut across the rope that held her wrist. She watched as Dawn rubbed her wounded forehead, getting up, but disoriented for a moment. "Hurry up, damn rope. Hurry up!" Bella kept cutting and cutting at the rope, all the while watching Dawn.

With another swift kick from her right leg, she knocked Dawn down again. This time, she stayed down. Finally, she was free of the rope and rushed over to Marco who was groaning and rubbing his head. He pulled something out of his back pocket: handcuffs. As Marco was disoriented, his eyes opening and closing, Bella grasped the handcuffs and cuffed Dawn while she was unconscious. She watched Dawn like a hawk to make sure she stayed unconscious. Bella leaned into Marco's arms, stroking his hair. Her body was weak and she could barely move. Police sirens sounded close by.

"The cavalry's here, but they're very late," Marco said.

Bella relished the warmth and safety of Marco's arms. "Thank you for saving me, Marco. I'd still be tied to the bed if it wasn't for you."

He managed a crooked smile. "I couldn't lose you."

Three weeks later, Bella sat on the couch at home with Marco while Jamie, Liz, and Claudia sat around them, watching the television news. After spending time in the hospital, giving her statement, and crime scene investigators processing Dawn's basement, she was arrested and awaiting trial. The amount of evidence found in the basement would put her in prison for the remainder of her natural life. She would never hurt anyone again. Bella was still recovering from her wounds and had started counselling with a psychologist specialising in childhood and adult trauma.

Liz turned to Bella. "So Jackson knew all about Mari killing women?"

Marco nodded. "Apparently so. He claimed loving her in his own dysfunctional way, and while he didn't agree with what she was doing, he couldn't turn her in either." He took a deep breath. "Jackson paid off a few people to keep his life in Perth and

Melbourne, a secret. It took a lot of digging and back-tracking, but we got there in the end."

Jamie shook her head. "A boyfriend's distorted love and all those women turned to dust. What a horrid shame."

"He tried to save me from her, but she couldn't let me go. To think we were friends in high school too. I never would've imagined her turning into this."

Marco held on to her hand. "I'm sorry. But I'm glad she's no longer around to stalk you or try to kill you again. We can get on with our lives."

"Amen to that," said Bella.

Claudia leaned forward. "I'm sorry you've been through all this, and I promise I will no longer give you a hard time."

"Thanks, Claudia. I appreciate that." After a calming breath, Bella turned to Marco, "How did you find me in that death place?"

"We traced medical records and found Mari's plastic surgeon in the city. She had plastic surgery not long after the fire, then changed her identity, making Dawn disappear. We questioned Jackson after the incident and offered him a deal; a reduced sentence in return for everything he knew about Dawn, or Mari, and his testimony in court. He said he never witnessed her kill anyone. That was a building they'd lived in temporarily after he took her in when her parents died, and never sold the place. He took care of her and was an adult when she met him. They became lovers. All these years they've had an open relationship. He confessed he suspected the kills, but never confronted her because of their special bond. He also didn't have evidence. After what she'd suffered at the hands of her parents, he wanted to make her forget her pain by living a free life."

Claudia shook her head. "That is so sick."

"So right," said Liz. "I still can't believe that sweet Mari was so depraved. Shocker."

Bella swallowed. "Not so surprising, given her true self. She was a narcissist and he was borderline. Both dysfunctional personalities that crave control and have a sense of entitlement." She fixed her gaze on Claudia. "Why did Mari attack you, Claudia?"

Claudia scoffed. "The bitch set me up with that necklace and got the police on to me. I was staring at her while I was waiting at your practice, telling myself that I had seen her somewhere before. She looked familiar to me, but it didn't hit me until later. I think it was her laugh when she took a phone call the time I visited you at your practice. That laugh reminded me of something. The day Marco questioned me after her attack, I realised I'd met Mari at Jackson's house. It was while he was my client, and I visited his home. She had her back turned and laughed when Jackson told me to get out of his house. It clicked that your receptionist and Jackson's girlfriend was the same person. She knew that I would eventually figure her out. If it wasn't for my friend ringing the doorbell, she would've kept stabbing me until I was dead."

Bella lost all breath. "I'm sorry you had to go through that."

Claudia frowned. "I can't imagine what that must've been like for you."

Marco nodded. "She'll be in prison for the rest of her life. Never getting out, and I'll make damn sure of that."

Chapter Sixty-One

SAFE AT LAST (SIX MONTHS LATER)

The light brown building with its arched windows and old-style presence of the Supreme Court suddenly lit up in Bella's eyes. Liz and Jamie wrapped their arms around Bella as Marco watched with a gleam in his eyes.

"Life imprisonment. Dawn got life without parole," said Bella.

"Yes, and thanks to your testimony," said Marco.

"I am happy for you girl. You are finally safe," said Liz.

"I couldn't be prouder of your absolute bravery," said Jamie.

"I say we go celebrate," said Bella.

Liz and Jamie stared at one another, then Liz said, "Jamie and I need to go. You and Marco catch up." She gave her a wink, and before Bella could respond, they both waved and rushed off.

"Let's go for a drink," Marco said.

Marco had been courting her for the last six months, taking her to fancy restaurants, the beach, day trips around Victoria, and to jazz bars. She was tired of him being nice and polite. "Let's go and have a drink at my place."

His eyes gleamed. "Okay, then. Lead the way."

Bella and Marco drove in their respective cars, and within half an hour, they had reached Bella's home. She unlocked the door and her hands shook as Marco followed behind her. Her breath weakened, and she perspired around her neck as she stepped into her home and placed her keys back in her bag.

When she turned around, Marco pushed her against the wall, kissing her deeply.

He pulled away with his hands around her waist. "We can finally be together gorgeous, knowing she'll never get out of prison."

Bella's face warmed. "Thanks to you for solving this case."

"I want us to have a future together, Bella. I love you."

Bella's mind turned to mush, knowing she felt exactly the same way. "I love you too."

She suddenly felt her face warm, her hands shaking from nerves. "I'll make us tea." She broke away and headed to the kitchen, her body quivering.

As she was filling up the mugs with teabags, she felt his warm, muscly arms wrap around her from behind. Bella turned, a magnetic pull drawing her to him as he smiled and grabbed her by the hand, pulling her to the bedroom. "Forget the tea then."

Gently, he pushed her on the bed and lay on top of her as they kissed hungrily. He pulled her t-shirt over her head and threw it to the floor.

Marco tenderly kissed her throat and trailed his mouth down to her breast. Gently he sucked her nipples as Bella moaned while stroking the back of his head. He shifted. "You are so beautiful. Are you sure you're ready for this?"

Bella nodded and brought her mouth to his. They dived into each other, devouring one another with desire. He pulled down Bella's loose pants, massaging the small of her back. He unclipped her bra and brought a nipple into his mouth as he sucked and kissed her breasts. Bella moaned and gently pushed his head further into her chest, highly aroused. Marco pulled back but she shook her head. "Don't stop."

He smiled. "I've waited so long for this." He caressed her inner thighs against her panties, and she wrapped her legs around him. She felt his hardness against his jeans. Marco's fingers tantalised her wetness underneath her underwear.

Their kiss deepened, tongues dancing, licking, and teeth gently biting. Bella touched his manhood, stroking it tenderly as she called out his name. "Oh, Marco."

He sounded out his arousal as he trailed slow kisses around her neck, shoulders and chest. His hands traced the outline of her breasts and glided down to her underwear. He prodded gently inside her panties with his fingers as Bella leaned in with her body while kissing her deeply, tantalising her with his teeth. He peeled off her panties but still kept his jeans on. When she was ready, he continued to probe her with his fingers. "I want you to orgasm, Bella. Let me see you come." He massaged her further as Bella found his erection over his jeans, stroking him too. She let herself go and climaxed.

Marco's tongue kept gliding in and out of her mouth. He took off his jeans, his body pressed against hers. He moved on top of her and lingered in his kiss for several minutes, teasing her further until Bella was aroused yet again. He entered her gently, moving himself against her until they screamed out their arousal close to each other.

Bella watched Marco sleep peacefully, like an angel. His stubble made him look sexy, and the hair over his eyes emitted a look of sweetness and innocence. He definitely wasn't innocent last night when they made love. He was wild, hungry, crazy, and delicious, and she couldn't get enough of him. Did she have regrets? Not at all, but she was afraid for the future. She couldn't believe he loved her, regardless of the warm sensation that filled her chest.

Marco stirred and, broken out of her reverie, Bella tucked the sheet over her chest. Suddenly, she was self-conscious of her body and her new scars.

"Hey there gorgeous. What a sight first thing in the morning. Come here you."

Bella blushed at his comment. She held on to the sheet and moved closer to Marco who wrapped his arm around her shoulder. She snuggled into the crook of his arm, a warm tingle running down her spine.

He shifted his body to face her then leaned in for a hungry kiss, their tongues gliding and delving deep into each others' mouths. "You don't know how long I've wanted to do this."

Bella beamed. "How long?"

He stroked her cheek. "Since the first day I met you, you had me. What about you?"

Bella's heart lifted. "That first day for me too. You were so in control in your role. So sexy in your Don Johnson detective clothing."

"Don Johnson, ha? That's a true compliment if I ever heard one."

Bella pulled apart. "Would you like breakfast?"

"Sure. I'll have you for breakfast." He leaned in for another kiss then pushed her towards the bathroom. He slid off her nightgown and took off his boxer shorts as they walked into the shower together. Turning on the water, Marco soaped Bella's body from top to bottom then she reciprocated. He brought her hands up over head and trailed kisses over her erect nipples, breasts, chest, and down to her inner thighs. His tongue pushed inside her wetness, probing and licking while his hands massaged her buttocks. Bella moaned in ecstasy and stroked the back of his head as he tantalised her until she exploded. He moved up. His mouth fell on top of hers in frenzied motion. He passionately penetrated her. His body hungered for hers as he pushed deeply into her and planted wet kisses around her breasts, massaging them with his hands. Within minutes, they both cried out in pleasure.

Chapter Sixty-Two

EPILOGUE – (TWO MONTHS LATER)

Bella lay nestled into Marco's arms as they watched a romantic comedy on TV. He gazed into her eyes at the end of the movie and leaned in for a kiss. He deepened the kiss when the doorbell rang.

Bella broke away and beamed at him. "Saved by the bell." She rose and headed to the door and stared up at Liz, whose hands were visibly shaking. "Liz, are you all right? Come in."

Liz stepped inside and cleared her throat. "My ex-boyfriend was released from prison and now I know he's going to find me."

Bella's chest tightened as the world around her washed away with the terror filling the air around them.

Reviews are gold to authors and allow Lucy to keep writing. If you enjoyed this story, please consider rating and reviewing it here: https://books2read.com/u/bw2ZeY

Check out and read 'Liz's Story' in the second book of the Friends In Crisis Series, *Twisted Obsession* here: https://books2read.com/u/4DW8pk

ABOUT THE AUTHOR

Lucy Appadoo is a prolific reader and author of the Friends In Crisis and Women of Strength Series. After a childhood spent reading and imagining escapist worlds, Lucy has put her imagination into stories. Her work as a rehabilitation counsellor, and former work as a counsellor in private practice, have led to an interest in writing inspirational stories about authentic, driven women who manage adversity with strength and heart. She writes in the genres of romantic suspense/thrillers with significant life themes and contemporary romance.

Lucy's interests include researching crime stories and news to inspire her work, watching crime thrillers and suspenseful movies, travel, exercising, reading for entertainment or knowledge, meditation, and spending time with friends and family. She also appreciates her Italian background and culture, which has inspired her to write imaginative stories about her parents' childhoods, leading to The Italian Family Series novels.

Check out Lucy's website and sign up for a FREE book here: www.lucyappadooauthor.com.au

ALSO BY LUCY APPADOO

<u>FICTION</u>
Women Of Strength Series – Romantic Suspense/Thriller
In Rio's Shadows (Book 1):
https://books2read.com/u/mq1qP8
Shadows Of The Past (Book 2):
https://books2read.com/u/3y1yAl

The Friends In Crisis Series - Romantic Suspense/Thriller
Haunted By The Past (Book 1):
https://books2read.com/u/bw2ZeY
Twisted Obsession (Book 2):
https://books2read.com/u/4DW8pk
Web Of Lies (Book 3):
https://books2read.com/u/3JXazE
Love-Obsessed (Book 4):
https://books2read.com/u/4jPKGX

The Hearts Series - Romantic Suspense
Rising Hearts (Book 1):
https://books2read.com/u/mZwpoE
Forbidden Hearts (Book 2):
https://books2read.com/u/bQBKr7
Kindred Hearts (Book 3):
https://books2read.com/u/4AJKQK
Broken Hearts (prequel novelette to Forbidden
Hearts): https://books2read.com/u/mgrnOD

Short Story Thrillers
Evening Interrupted:
https://books2read.com/u/3yZDjZ
The Dreamcatcher:
https://books2read.com/u/bzaLxn
Red Flags:https://books2read.com/u/bWZ9W1
Collection of Short Story Thrillers:
https://books2read.com/u/bP5vwj

**The Italian Family Series - Coming of Age
Family Drama/Romance**
A New Life: https://books2read.com/u/mqqwZm
The Beauty of Tears:
https://books2read.com/u/bpqwk3
Dancing in the Rain:
https://books2read.com/u/bOr7LA
A Life By Design: https://books2read.com/u/3J8ene

<u>NON-FICTION</u>
Grief & Loss:
Moving Beyond Grief - How To Shift
From Grief & Loss to Joy & Peace:
https://books2read.com/u/mVNzDA

Stress Management & Anxiety
Holistic Spiritual and Mental Health -
Building Resilience and Creativity by
Conquering Anxiety and Managing Stress:
https://books2read.com/u/47kG8A

Career Guidance
Your Holistic Career Path - Create Career
Change, Satisfaction, and Work/Life Balance:
https://books2read.com/u/bzYDz4